I0690596

Steve's First Job

First Edition

Published by The Nazca Plains Corporation
Las Vegas, Nevada
2009

ISBN: 978-1-935509-20-2

Published by

The Nazca Plains Corporation ®
4640 Paradise Rd, Suite 141
Las Vegas NV 89109-8000

PUBLISHER'S NOTE
Steve's First Job is a work of fiction created wholly by **Pete Brown**'s
imagination. All characters are fictional and any resemblance to any
persons living or deceased is purely by accident. No portion of this
book reflects any real person or events.

Cover Photo, Mircea Netea
Art Director, Blake Stephens

Steve's First Job

First Edition

Pete Brown

PART I

When I was a lot younger I seemed to have more time. There always seemed to be time to talk to my buddies on the phone, or, when they went away to college, to type them long e-mails. In spite of all my aides and secretaries, I never seem to have time for any of this stuff now - it's tougher at the top that most people think. But last weekend I was clearing out the private files on my PC - the very private ones, that not even my trusted executive assistant is allowed access to - when I came across some old copies of notes I'd sent to my then best buddy, Stu, when he'd gone off college in Atlanta.

As I read them, it took me right back to those early, more innocent days, right after the war when there was still some degree of chaos as the states sorted out their new responsibilities and the two new governments set themselves up in Chicago and Denver. Stu and I hadn't been affected, fortunately: the war finished just as we were about to be drafted, at sixteen, so we didn't have to slog around the country fighting the North as so many young men from our high school had to. And with the fighting over and the truce in place, it was much easier for rich and influential men like my father, and Stu's, to buy us exemptions from the draft - or perhaps they had to buy a couple of slaves and send them in our place, or pay a bounty, or something: it's all detail, and I forget.

Anyway, at the time of these notes Stu was just away in Atlanta, as I've said, and I was still arguing with my father about why I couldn't join him. "Look, Steve", he told me sternly. "It's not a matter of the money, you know that. But I need you in the business. You need to learn about it properly. You'll inherit all the demesne one day, and its associated businesses, and it's large and complex. If you don't start getting to grips with it, you'll be wasting your inheritance."

"But dad, Stu went.... What about their holdings? Isn't their demesne much the same size as ours?"

"Yes, and Stu has several brothers already working in their business. Let him enjoy college now, as I think he'll have a tough time later on - younger brothers don't usually do well in family businesses, you know. I wouldn't be surprised if your buddy ended up as a doctor, or lawyer, or something.... Not as one of the owners of a demesne, as you will be."

"But dad..."

"Steve, I don't want to hear any more. You will either do as I say, or leave now, leave totally, and go and make your own way in the world. Your mother left you a small inheritance from her own fortune - the part that didn't come to me on marriage - and that should be enough to get you started. But don't expect any support form me unless you're going to act like a dutiful son should, and take your proper place in the order of things, and knuckle down and get stuck into our business!"

"But dad..."

"No more, Steve. Get to work, or get out. Make your own mind up."

Well, I'd half a mind to just walk out, go to the train station, and buy a ticket to "somewhere". Dad and I are both incredibly strong willed and I knew there was no shaking him, and I was really pissed off and ought to have gone my own way. But it's hard at eighteen, especially when you've always had the finer things in life: my own suite in the big house, my own personal slave to look after all my clothes and stuff... Sure, times had been difficult during the war, but the supply of the good things in life had never been much affected where we were deep down in Tennessee: it was annoying not to be able to travel to all the "fun" places like New York and San Francisco as we had done when I was a child, when mom was still alive, before the war started: she was not really "of the south", as dad was, and relished those trips "to civilisation, to catch up on the plays, the music, the art....", as she put it.

More than most of my contemporaries, I suppose, because of these trips I knew how expensive things could be out there in the real world, and how unpleasant things could be without slaves to take away most of the irritations of modern life. Much as I wanted to show dad that I was at least as capable as he was at making my own decisions, in the end common sense prevailed and I stayed at home. And then dad began his programme of introducing me to the businesses on which our family's fortunes were based.

I'd forgotten most of this stuff, and it was only finding this old copy of my notes to and from Stu that brought it rushing back: it's a miracle that the software still existed to read them after all these years, and I sat there for half an hour as I pored over the display, reliving those few weeks in my life. I think it will be interesting for my grandchildren to know how it was in those days before the almost universal use of "bred" slaves swept away some of the practices of the day, and so I've copied and reproduced those exchanges of e-mail here. If I had more time, I suppose I could add comments to them, or give them a definitive time line, but I think that as a "taster" of how things were, they are sufficient in themselves. All those interested can of course always access the national archives, with all the news bulletins, documentaries, films and such like from those days.

So here it is, after all those years, just as it was written.

Stu, you old dog! How are the bitches in Atlanta? I know you - be careful: some of those sophisticated city ladies won't be expecting a country-boy cocksman like you, and will swoon when you start some of those tricks we both learned on the black girls from our demesnes. On the other hand, old buddy, they might have tricks you might not be on the look out for: they do say that they deliberately get in the family way, and then expect you to marry them; and if you won't, they take your folks to court and sue for megabucks. I can't imagine your dad would be pleased about that... And he might even decide it would be cheaper to let you get sold off as a slave. Still, don't worry: if that looks likely just tip me the wink and I'll make sure I buy you - I've always fancied your ass, as I've told you, but you've never let me in. As a slave, you'd have no choice. Write to me, and tell me what it's like in the big wide world out there - I feel stifled down here sometimes. Steve.

Steve: God, it's so formal here in Atlanta. A jacket and tie is required all the time in college. And if I "date" a young lady, as they call themselves, it's a suit, especially if we "visit with" her parents, as they call it. No more jeans and Ts for me. They say it's so we are distinguished from the slaves, who are dressed "for work". Unlike back home where the blacks only work in the fields and around the house, slaves here do all kinds of stuff - in offices, stores... You even see slaves managing other slaves. You often can't tell at first, especially as some of them are whiteys, and I've sometimes made the mistake of saying "thank you" when a slave has served me in a store: I was with a few guys from my frat once when I did this, and they almost screamed the place down with their laughter. It seems they have a sixth sense for who's a slave, and don't have to keep looking for the collars, as I do. The women around here just don't put it around - unless, as I said, you "visit with" their folks, and practically get engaged... And then god help you if you don't go through with it. Fortunately the frat has a few slaves up in the attics.... But especially on the weekends they're very heavily used and although I know we're supposed to be frat brothers and all that, I'm not sure I like using a slave when she's still slimy with my "brother's" spunk. Thanks for the warning, though - I'll make sure I don't get enslaved: the thought of that big d ck of yours forcing its way into my tight hole doesn't bear thinking about - it's making me wince even as I type this. Still, there are enough blacks on your demesne that your dick isn't lacking in exercise, I assume? Take care, buddy... Stu.

Stu: Don't worry about your hole, old buddy. If you were a slave of mine I'd soon get you nicely stretched and you'd be panting for your owner to service you. Especially as I'd keep your dick in a chastity cage so you couldn't fuck or even jerk yourself off - the only time you'd get relief would be when my dick massaged your prostate. Must go now, as dad is sending me off to work in our hauliers - it's one of our most profitable businesses, and he wants me to learn the ropes. It sounds a bit dodgy, though: instead of going to the Board meetings and stuff, he wants me to work with some old-timer in charge of procurement, and "work my way up". It sounds a stupid way of doing things to me: owners should manage and set strategic directions for the business, not become involved in the day to day detail. Still, after the huge row with dad about college, I've got to humour him a bit. I'm pretending to go along with what he says so that when I want six months off to go and see Europe I can point out that I've done everything that he's asked me to. Will you come with me? Those foreigners might be pretty peculiar, and I'd like my old buddy close by - very close by - to help me. We could share a bed, and you don't have to take my dick - well, except in your hand. I do miss those mutual jerk-offs. Steve.

Stu: Hey, it was good to chat on the phone. I do understand why you can't come to Europe as you'll have to work in the vacations from Atlanta - folks can be a real pain, can't they, always trying to stop guys having a bit of fun? Anyway, my dad got me started today, and what a day! I kind of thought I might be in the office or something, but when I got to the depot downtown and spoke to the receptionist, she activated a pager, and this really old guy eventually came out to meet me. Well, I say "old" - he was probably only forty! But he had a hard, mean look and he was clearly used to working physically, as he packed tight jeans and a T, and those tan leather work boots with thick soles. He shook my hand - it was kind of hard with patches of tough skin on it, and he squeezed me as if he was testing me: I'm glad we did all those workouts in the gym as I think I gave back as good as I got. His name's Jon, and he seems to be some sort of supervisor at the depot - not the manager, who does sit in the office, but the guy down there "on the shop floor", who actually runs things. Not really knowing what to expect, I'd worn my new dress chinos, my designer leather casuals, a smart shirt, and had a jacket in deep tan linen, and the first thing he said was "Boy, you'd better go home and change: we've got to go off to the military today, and the men there can be pretty rough on someone who's dressed fancy". And that was it. I'm just dashing this off to you as I change - I guess I can't go wrong if I follow his lead, so I've pulled on my faded jeans - the ones you laugh about as the bottoms are all frayed - but which I like as they're so snug and I think they show me off to good advantage. And that plain dark grey T you gave me last Christmas. See ya later. I'd better dash back, as that Jon looks pretty businesslike. Steve.

Stu: Wow! What a day. Jon told me that my dad wanted me to see the business "from the bottom up". As you know, we're big in logistics and distribution, and the depot services the last leg of the thing - the big trucks come in and the loads are broken up for the locals, and deliveries take place from there. We use drays, mostly, as the costs are pretty much unbeatable compared with stuff powered by gasoline or diesel since the huge price hikes. Anyway, the depot's expanding and we were to go and buy and train a new set of dray animals, and then I'm going to use them deliveries for the next few months - so long to Europe, I guess! Jon and I were going to the big base on the outskirts of town, but when we went outside and I went to get into my trap, he was almost offended. "You can't go in that, Steve!", he told me, "They'll think you're some rich guy and hike the prices. Anyway, the government usually provides transportation back, and you'll want to be with the animals. So I had to send Blackie home by himself - the lazy fucker didn't even run as he set off, and if this behaviour persists he'll need a good whipping. Then we caught the street car out to the base - I haven't been on one of those for years and it's quite interesting, actually, to see all the other folk riding, going about their business.

The streetcar stops four blocks from the base - you probably remember it, as when we were kids they used it for training marines, and there were all those hunky guys around who we used to like to look at. Now, though, since the war, they've turned it over to keeping the POWs. They're all under normal military discipline as they say that's the easiest way to keep them under control - they're mostly self-policing, with their own officers and stuff, and it's only the perimeter that needs guarding. Mind you, it's pretty grim as you approach it: several layers of high wire fencing w th that "razor" stuff all over it to stop them escaping, and guard towers with machine guns - you can see they mean business. You can just make out the POWs exercising as you walk up the drive - it' funny, really, as it's so impeccably neat, with all the stones along the edge of the drive painted white. There are guards on the gates, of course - our soldiers, obviously, and they checked our ID and let us in, pointing out that we wanted the "sales" building, rather than "Base Admin".

You kind of expect military stuff to be all drab and green or grey, but the sales building was different: more like a Realtors, with big green plants, spotlights, comfortable chairs in front of modern desks. Our sales advisor was a guy in his twenties in a good suit, and when we sat down he asked us what we were looking for. Jon looked at me, as I'm supposed to be picking and choosing, but I had no idea. So I asked him to specify our requirements, and he rapped out pretty smartly "Nine. Not younger than twenty two, as we need them to have properly developed bodies. Not older than thirty two, as we want them to have a long working ife after we've trained them. Tall. Muscular - prefer heavy set, as it's powerful work they have to do, rather than something for speed. Cart horse, rather than race horse, as you might say. That's about it, really."

I wondered about the nine, as our drays are usually pulled by teams of eight, but Jon clearly knew the ropes, so I said nothing. They asked us to wait and there were comfortable couches with the Wall Street

Journal, Newsweek, and all that sort of stuff, and a young slave came and took our orders for complimentary coffees, and Danish.

Our sales associate collected us after only twenty minutes or so, and told us the stock was ready for inspection, and we followed him through the base towards one of the huts that were lined up in neat rows - all very military. As we went, we saw groups of the POWs exercising: some groups were drilling, marching up and down and stuff, and some were out doing what looked like heavy-duty physical jerks, all under the control of their own officers, as I've told you. The sales associate told us that they were kept like that, with normal military discipline maintained, as it not only ensured the men kept fit and healthy, but it required far fewer of our soldiers to act as guards and stuff as the POWs were usually so tired that they had little energy to try to escape.

The hut we went in to was almost bare inside, but they'd lined up the stock already and they were waiting for us - at least twenty guys, in what remained of their military uniforms: mostly camo pants, and khaki Ts, and army boots. Some of them must have been fresh from those exercise fields, as their Ts were stained with sweat, and overall there was that "male" smell about the place that you get in sports clubs and stuff - sweat, piss, testosterone.... well, you know. I felt myself getting hard - not just from the smell and the sight of these fit, muscular guys, but because I was going to actually select them! Jon looked expectantly at me, and I kind of shrugged. "Shall I help you pick, then, son?" He asked. He'd called me "son" several times, and I hated it - I mean, he's only about twenty years older than me, and I am actually the son of his employer, and I think a bit of respect is due. Still, I did need his help, as I haven't a fucking clue about what to look for, so I told him to go ahead.

We went along the line of men and he made some simple choices first. There were five black guys, and he rejected all of them. He says that he's not personally prejudiced, but blacks can be awkward, especially blacks from the North who have lived almost like ordinary men before being called up into their army. And he says there are some prejudiced guys around, and it can be more difficult to get proper "bonding" in the team with a black in it, as some of the others don't like having to work with blacks. There were three Asiatics, too - big, tough guys who were initially probably from Korea or somewhere like that - not little Thai boys, as we'd specified height and strength. They got rejected as he says that when the going gets really tough towards the end of a long day, with tight deadlines to meet for the last few deliveries, they tend to collapse under the whip and don't respond to it properly. I guess he knows best, from his experience.

So that left us twelve to pick from, although I guess they'd bring more in if these were not suitable. We walked slowly along the back of the line then, and he pointed out something I've never really thought about before - all the POWs were about the same height, six two to six four, but they were differently proportioned: their waists came at very different heights as some had long legs and short bodies, some long bodies and relatively short legs, and so on. We were apparently looking for "good balance" as you need good long legs for the pulling, but a lot of that strength is wasted if they haven't got good, big sound lungs to power the whole thing. He rejected six on this count, and so we had too few, and we indeed did have to wait around whilst the sales associate shouted orders out of the door, and ten more POWs were marched in.

Jon was pretty fussy I'll say that for him, and he seemed to know what he was looking for. Occasionally he'd run his hands over the flanks or the butt of one of the POWs, and I wished he'd have offered to show me what he was looking for - it would have been good to get my hands on that strong, male flesh. But there were enough complaints from the men as it was as he did this, and he looked rather cross. "We'll" soon teach them proper manners, once we're at the depot", he told me rather curtly.

Finally, we had twelve who were "mostly up to standard" as Jon called it, and then he told the sales associate to have them strip so we could get a proper look at the bodies. They didn't like doing this, you could tell, but the sales guy threatened them with a standard slave prod that he had clipped to his belt, and they all complied, but with a lot of grumbling, and they stood there in their army cotton boxers in khaki, and their socks. I was embarrassed as my dick was rock solid now, seeing all their bodies starting to get displayed, and in those jeans there's just no hiding it! Jon went up and down the line, front and back, again, and a couple were rejected as they had "unsightly" tattoos on places like their calves, and shoulders. Jon said that small tattoos - arm bands, "semper fi" for the marines, that kind of stuff, was acceptable mostly, as the public knew that most slaves were ex soldiers, but anything too big, or in an unsuitable place meant rejection as they'd be going around the streets for our company and we needed to keep up standards.

He looked at me then and said "Well, there's ten here, which nine shall we take?". I honestly didn't know - they all looked much alike to me, so I asked him how we could tell. "Well, if all else fails, there's always the dick test", he said, smiling, and asked the sales associate to have the men made totally naked. Some of them really protested at this, and I saw Jon making what looked like a mental note of these potential trouble makers. And the sales associate actually had to unclip his prod and wave it around in front of a couple of them before they all dropped their boxers and stood there to totally nude except for their socks. I was in big trouble now - I felt certain there'd be a damp patch on my jeans as I was leaking so much pre-cum at the sight of all these hunky bodies. But even I could see which one to reject then - he was outstanding, or, rather, to totally underwhelming! Actually his dick wasn't all that tiny, but compared to the size of his body, it just looked ridiculous. He must have been used to being teased about it, though, as he just shrugged when Jon said that we didn't want one with a kid's dick like that.

So then we had our nine. The sales associate asked us to accompany him back to the sales hut to draw up the contracts, and the men went to start dressing - but Jon said that wasn't necessary. "Just boots and tags" he told the sales associate: the tags so we can register them properly before we collar them, and the boots as their feet aren't tough enough yet until we have them trained. My dick gave another jerk at the thought that we could order these big tough guys around just like that, and I felt like asking Jon if we hadn't better see if they could all shoot a good load - that would have been a real sight. But he'd moved off, and I wasn't sure about what exactly we could, and could not, ask to see.

There's quite a lot of paperwork, actually: you need the POWs name and army serial number, and all that kind of stuff, and they won't accept credit cards or anything: Jon had got a certified cheque before we left the office, as he knew the ropes, but we'd have been in trouble without that. I guess it's a bit like buying a used automobile from a dealer's lot - you don't trust him until you've seen the registration papers, and he doesn't trust anything other than a certified bank cheque (or cash, I suppose) for payment.

Jon was grumbling about the price being so high, when there were so many POWs available, but the sales associate had what seemed like the "approved" government answer "We've got tens of thousands of these northern POWs and we can't release them all on to the market simultaneously as prices would collapse and many free men would be put out of work. It's the government's policy to release new stock in an orderly, controlled rate that the market can bear, and in the meantime the other POWs have to be guarded, housed, fed, and so on. The price you pay reflects this, and the government thanks you for your support." So there! It was only afterwards that it occurred to me that I ought to have asked why the POWs just couldn't be repatriated back to the north, as you usually do after a war. But I suppose it's because a civil war causes all kinds of different problems, and it might mean that those pesky northerners might again try to stop us living our own lives in the way we've chosen.

It seems that the price included transportation "a reasonable distance" and after everything was signed and sealed we went outside and saw a small standard carriage cage on the back of a flatbed truck. The nine we'd chosen were then herded out of the hut we'd been in by guards with guns, and once they saw they were to go into the cage, some of our purchases started to protest - mostly because they said they weren't slaves, but POWs, but a couple because they didn't want to be carried through the streets naked. It's as if the whole thing had started to become real to them at that point - or perhaps it's the odd sensation of being naked out of doors, - you know how it is, like when we went camping that time, and we felt so strange even when there weren't any other folks around for miles. One was so violent that they actually did use a slave prod on him and the soldiers then picked up his twitching body and just threw it into the cage, and the rest them followed, although very reluctantly.

The driver was a young soldier and I sat between him and Jon as we drove out of the base and back towards our depot. I asked him if he liked being a guard there, and he said it was better than actually fighting: some of it had been pretty brutal in the northern cities before they finally surrendered when their oil ran out (most of the oil fields are in the south of course) and the electricity was cut from those big generators on the southern rivers. "I guess that if the war had gone the other way you might have been in a POW camp in the north, and you might have been in the cage at the back, rather than up front, driving", I joked. "Hey, it's not such a bad life for them, and I don't know I'd mind all that much", he told me. "I've got a wife and two kids to support on army pay, and that's pretty tough. At least those guys have got rid of all that baggage and are free to be themselves." I wondered what he meant by that, and Jon explained that most of the stock we bought was that bit older as we didn't buy the POWs who were "raw recruits". So ours were mostly "career" soldiers, and the culture of the army meant that you had a family and such like.

We got back to the depot and Jon made sure there were a number of our own handlers, all with slave prods at the ready, before the cage was opened and they were allowed to clamber out - slowly and carefully, as they weren't used to climbing around naked and were evidently worried about their balls! We moved them immediately into one of the over-night sleeping cages where the teams are kept, and once the door was securely locked, Jon gave an almost audible sigh of relief. "It's the most difficult time for a slave, Steve", he told me. "Look, they were all soldiers, then POWs. They kind of knew - knew intellectually, if you like - that they'd be sold as slaves one day, but they've been in that base for over a year waiting, and it didn't happen, and they must have started to think it never would. Now it has, and they haven't adjusted and still think of themselves as soldiers, and soldiers try to escape, and to fight. So it's a dangerous time for us - and them - until we can start convincing them that their life has changed, changed utterly. It's best we keep them here tonight and start fresh tomorrow - but they're your team, your responsibility now - make sure they're comfortable. You need to do that every night, so your team bonds with you and learns that you're responsible for them." I asked him what was to be done, and he looked a bit exasperated, as if it ought to be obvious - but how the fuck was I supposed to know what you do with a bunch of naked slaves? At home, our own guards look after all that stuff. "First, have they got enough bedding? Just check the straw in there and make sure there's enough to keep their bodies off the bare concrete. Secondly, is the water spigot working? Just flick the tongue plate up and down - you can reach it through the bars - so that when they need to drink, there's clean water available. And you also feed them, but we'll skip that tonight, as they'll react better if they're hungry tomorrow."

It was a real pain getting home, as I've told you I sent Blackie back earlier with my trap. So I had to go on the streetcar again, and it was rush hour. I don't know how all the poor folk manage every day - we were packed in like cattle. Steve.

Steve: Well, old buddy, you seem to be turning into a real live 100% slave driver. Look, we've debated this before, and I don't want it to come between us. But you know that my whole family is opposed to slavery - dad even imports Mexicans to work our demesne, and mom and dad don't much like me being buddies with you at the best of times. They almost forbad me to see you that summer when you came over and saw me cutting the grass, and offered to go back and fetch one of your dad's slaves to do it as it wasn't "dignified" for a free man to be doing work like that. So if you meet mom or dad, just chat politely and ask how I'm doing - that will fill the time, as they're really proud that I got a scholarship here; and for fuck's sake don't tell them about how you're getting on at work! They say that the northern POWs are just that, POWs, and entitled to be treated as soldiers, who need "rehabilitating" but then repatriating back to their homes and families in the north. Their church has cake sales and collections to raise money to advertise for the anti-slavery society, you know that! Anyway, take care. I've met a stunning girl whose over here from Sweden - she's so much more relaxed about "things" than our southern girls, and I'm confident I'll get my leg over tonight. Must rush - I need to shower, so I'm fresh and sweet. Stu.

Stu: Chasing tail, as ever! I was expecting an up to date progress report this morning, but as I had nothing from you I expect you did the dirty deed and managed to stay over at her place? Take care, buddy - you don't want to get lumbered until you've had time to play the field a bit more... But maybe it's too late for that anyway? They say those European women all take the pill, so perhaps you'll be OK. I always thought it was a crap idea to ban contraception for the unmarried as it would reduce promiscuity - sometimes our southern senators can be real assholes when it comes to logic, and they are too much influenced by the church, who are a real bunch of killjoys. But is it true they don't shave their pits, or legs... Or anywhere?

I drove Blackie down to the depot this morning as I couldn't face the streetcar again, but mindful of what Jon had said about not being "different", I sent him home when I was a couple of blocks form the depot. It was still very early (at least for me!), but Jon was already there as he has a small apartment that's kind of part of our compound - a lot of the single guys find it's good to live right on the spot, and dad encourages it by making worker accommodation available at very reasonable rentals - he says the men are then on hand in case of problems, and the money he loses on the low rentals he saves from not having to have a lot of guys on "stand by" and "call out", and he doesn't have to pay cab fares to get them home if the shifts overrun or anything.

Jon led me through into the barns where the slaves live, and "my" group were still asleep, mostly, sprawled out all across each other on the straw. Jon says that we deliberately keep them in small cages so that they can't avoid each other, and can't help being in close contact with each other's bodies - it helps them to "bond" properly as a team. He banged on the bars of their cage with his prod, and it was comical, almost, as they scrambled to their feet: most of them still had their morning hard-on, and when they realised it, they tried to cover themselves with their hands. It's funny - some of them came awake almost immediately, and some of them were yawning and rubbing their eyes for two or three minutes. Just like ordinary guys, really. And, as guys do when they wake up, some of them were scratching their balls, and some their pits. Jon said to me that a lot of this would be fixed later in the day.

Jon told them all to have a good drink as they wouldn't be getting any more water for a long time, and we had to wait as they all knelt down in turn in front of the spigot and press their mouths around it to release the water. One of them asked Jon when they were going to be fed, and he snapped that slaves didn't ask questions - they just waited, and sooner or later, when their handlers were ready, they'd be fed. He turned to me and told me that for the first few weeks we deliberately changed feeding times at random, and sometimes skipped meals altogether, feeding them double the next time: it apparently helps the slaves to realise that they're no longer in charge of even simple things like that, and that they're totally dependent on us.

It was a bit gross then, as it was time for them to piss and crap - they weren't used to the idea that slaves just crouch down and do it over a hole direct into the sewers. I guess Jon was ready for it, though, as he'd lined up some of the other handlers, with their slave prods at the ready, so there was no trouble. He whispered to me as we watched them do their business that this morning was the really difficult part - by the time we'd finished with them and they were all collared and so on, they'd have started to adjust to their new status and would be much easier to handle.

It seems the depot deals with a fair few new slaves, so we have the facilities on site, rather than needing to send the slaves out for processing. The best thing of all is the "cramp", that keeps the slaves secure during processing: it's just two lines of bars, really, just a couple of feet apart so the slaves can only line up one behind the other and can't get out of line or anything. There's a gate at one end so you can take the next slave off the front of the line, and it's a bit like an airlock as only one slave at a time can get through. Similarly, at the other end there's another arrangement of gates so you can return a slave there after processing. But in addition to that there's a kind of moveable plate that slides along rails on both sides of the rows of bars - you can push this from the back towards the front from the outside and thus "cramp" the slaves together. I couldn't understand this at first, but its use became obvious as the morning progressed.

The handlers directed the slaves into the cramp, and then the first one was pulled out of the gate at the front. He stood there in his army boots and dog tags, and Jon directed him over to kneel in front of an anvil thing, with a hollow for his neck in it. He was very suspicious, but kept a wary eye on Jon's slave prod so it seems they all know what happens if one of these touches your bare skin. There's a full-time blacksmith in the depot as there's always work to do with the slaves or the dray carts and he went over and measured the slave's neck, then fetched a collar, slipped it under the neck in the hollow in the anvil, then used a "shaping tool", I suppose you'd call it, that fitted in to the anvil and allowed the collar to be bent in a smooth curve, to close it up. There's a lot of noise and some sparks fly as he uses a red-hot rivet to close the collar permanently, and it's quite a sight to watch: it's perfectly humane, though, as there's a bit of wet sacking thrown over the slave's shoulders so he isn't burned by the sparks. The blacksmith is a real sight, too - a huge, muscular guy, with biceps that stand out almost like footballs as he wields the hammer or strains to bend the collar - he just wears a leather apron to cover his front and protect him, but his back is to totally bare and you can see the sweat running down his back and funnelling into his ass crack. The slaves at home all have thin, stainless steel collars, but the ones at the depot working on the drays have the conventional thick, heavy black cast iron ones, riveted on, as I've explained. Jon said that firstly it looks more reassuring for the pub ic to see slaves heavily collared like that, and secondly that these big men need thick, heavy collars so that everything is in "proportion" - actually, I think he's right: those thing stainless steel things would look too frail on these big guys, even though they're probably just as strong and as difficult to remove.

When the slave was allowed to stanc up he seemed surprised by the weight of the collar, and his head was slightly bowed. But then there was nearly trouble, as the blacksmith reached up and cut through the thin chain holding his dogtags on, and tossed them into a bin. The slave protested, and Jon almost had to drive him back to the cramp and in through the rear gates. "See, Steve, the realisation is beginning to set in", he told me as we watched the blacksmith take the next slave from the front of the line. "Whilst they still have their dogtags, they can still think of themselves as soldie-s. Now he's beginning to realise that he's just a common slave, collared like all slaves are."

With all the collars securely in place, Jon asked me what I wanted to do about the hair on my team. Well, I had no idea. So I asked for his advice - always a good thing to do, as I was finding out. "It's a difficult one, Steve", he told me. "You're a fashionab e kind of guy, judging from those clothes you turned up in on the first day, and that pony you had on your trap had the fashionable 'naked' look, I noticed. You have him totally shaved,, right?" So I told him t1at yes, I did have Blackie completely shaved as "Gentleman's Quarterly" had said that this was all the rage in New Orleans and the other fashionable places. I'd wanted it permanently removed with electrolysis, but dad had a fit when I told him how much it would cost just to do Blackie's balls, let alone his head. "Well that's OK for your personal pony, I guess", Jon said, "But it's a lot of work here - you'd have to wait around all the time, supervising them, to make sure they shaved off every scrap of stubble almost every day. Don't you find it a problem with your pony?" I shrugged and pointed out that at home we have a stockman to take care of things like that, and he just laughed! "No time for all those idlers, Steve. You're the 'stockman' for your team, so unless you want to spend a lot of time monitoring them, I'd say the naked look was totally out - mind you, it does help the bonding between the team and their driver, as running your hands all over their skulls and bodies every day gets them to accept your touch. But if I were you, I'd go for a compromise look: head hair at half an inch, as most of them have that anyway from the marines, but with no sideburns and with the napes cut crisply in a sharp line. Loose all their pit hair - they'll sweat a lot as they're working and as they lift the crates and stuff on and off the dray, it's more aesthetic than showing a big ugly patch of wet hair. You only need scrape it clear every week or so, so it's not too difficult to manage. Then the pubes and so on - well, I always think all slaves' balls should be shaved, as it makes them look tidier and of course we are going to 'ring' them and that's harder when their balls are all hairy. And most of them have really unruly pubic thatches, that's most unsightly So I'd recommend you have them much reduced, to a nice neat patch just above their dicks, and then have that trimmed to no more than half an inch. As for the rest - well, personally I think a bit of variety is nice, seeing all the different combinations of colours and shading and growth on their pecs, bellies, arm and legs, so I'd leave well alone.".

Look, I don't want to bore you with all of this, and it's getting late as it took a fair old time to get them all properly trimmed and so on.... There was a lot of complaints as they were shorn and shaved, but Jon told me to ignore it as we don't listen to slaves, and it just showed that they were starting to realise that their lives had changed for ever when another guy could order their pubes to be clipped! But nothing prepared me - or them, I suppose, for the branding, as I'll tell you about tomorrow! But tell me - was she all hairy, and do you want my advice about the management of body hair? I must be starting to be an expert. Steve.

Steve: Look, buddy, I know you're trying to be humorous, but please don't compare my girlfriend with your slaves. Not even in jest, OK? And to answer your question from yesterday, no she doesn't shave her pits! But it's actually quite erotic, as there's another place to sniff and lick. Look, Steve, I don't think it's good for you to be around all these slaves, as you seem to be losing some of that sensitivity that makes you such a nice guy to be buddies with. You don't have to work for your dad, you know- you can always get a job elsewhere. Or why don't you tap some of the other members of that big sprawling family of aunts, uncles and cousins of yours and get to a college? At least with a proper education you could make your own way in the world. Stu

PART2

Stu: Well, if seeing the slaves shaved and collared in the morning wasn't erotic enough, in the afternocn we moved on to having their brands burned in. I know it's controversial, but it is the law - I mean, how else, ultimately, can you tell a slave from a free man if you can't see his brand? An escaped slave can always have his collar removed, or a tattoo effaced, but there's no way of getting rid of the deep scarring from the branding. Anyway, I know we've talked about it in the past and you think it's cruel, but that isn't the point: it's the law, and owners who don't have it done face extremely heavy fines, and even imprisonment. Jon says that branding is good for the slaves, though: once they understand that they are so totally in our power that we can order the mutilation of their bodies in this way, it brings home to them that their life has changed irrevocably and that they're now no longer "men". They might entertain the hope that one day some change in their circumstances would lead to their freedom and they could have their collars cut off and return to "normal" life, but the fact that we can order them to be branded signals clearly and finally to them that this is never going to happen. A slave's hide, marked with an ownership mark, is so clearly "property", just like we have the china in the workers' canteen marked to prevent them stealing it.

Jon said that the branding would best be done after we'd eaten, as the stench of the burning skin could upset the stomach, so we left the slaves in the "crush" and went over to the canteen - but not before we'd used the moveable barrier at the rear of it to really "crush" the slaves up tight against each other, so that their dicks were lodging in the butt cracks of the guy in front, and their bodies were in contact along their whole length. We just left them there and went off - they couldn't escape from the barred "crush" after all - and Jon said it was another part of the bonding that they needed to go through: in our forty minute lunch break it was inevitable that some of them would bone up, and they'd start to overcome their shyness and embarrassment at knowing that their fellows could feel it.

Our company treats its workers well and the canteen for the depot workers is subsidised - again, dad says that it's only common sense, as with cheap, good food the workers stay there during their lunch breaks and only use their forty minutes. If we didn't do this, they'd go out, it might take longer, and they might end up in bars and so on and come back with a drink or two inside them, which would lower productivity. Dad's good like that, understanding how to make a "win-win" situation that's good for the men and good for the company.

The slaves don't eat lunch, though: they're fed twice a day, normally, although as I've explained, during their initial training we vary this a bit so that they learn to understand their total dependency on us for everything. Jon said it was a good idea to water them before the branding started, though, and he insisted I do this. "They're your team, Steve, and they need to learn that it's from you that their sustenance comes. Think of it like training a dog - a good owner always feeds a new dog himself, so it knows that the hand that feeds him is his master's." So I went down the line of them as they stood there in the "crush" with the waterer - that's what we use most of the time: it's a big bag of water on a strap, that you sling over your shoulders an under one arm, with a pipe coming out of it. You put the pipe in the slave's mouth, then squeeze your arm down to force the water up and into him. It's a pretty standard way of doing it, as it ensures no water is wasted because everything goes into the slave's mouth. Some of them wanted to refuse the water, but Jon had warned me not to allow this. "They're worried about having tc piss in the "crush", Steve. But a slave needs water to be able to work properly, and they've got to learn that when their master gives them some, they take it: if you start to let a slave make decisions for himself, you're on the top of a slippery slope where soon it's him who's deciding everything, not you." Mind you, I didn't like having to force their mouths open to get the pipe in.

I don't know what it must be like to get an erection when you're standing so close to the guy in front that your dick forces its way between his butt cheeks, but it can't be all that bad, surely? But when one guy started to piss after the watering, a whole lot of shouting and argument broke out. Well, what else could the poor guy do? And it's not as if there's a real problem with piss, is there - I mean, it's perfectly sterile. Still, I suppose the first time you feel a stream of hot piss bursting in your butt crack it must be a bit unsettling.

The slaves all started to look really worried when they brought in the branding kit - a stout frame, to tie the slaves down on to, the same slave who'd collared them that morning, and a glowing charcoal brazier which he tends. Jon told me that it is now possible to brand slaves with a branding iron dipped in liquid nitrogen or some such, but that we prefer the "traditional" way as the heat, the smell of the searing flesh and the sizzling sound as the branding iron burns its way through the skin and subcutaneous fat layers all add to the atmosphere and remind the slave that this is it, this is his life from now on.

The first slave in line in the crush, the first one who was going to be branded therefore, was a blond guy - big boned, open faced, bright blue eyes, and with a shock of curly dirty blond hair before he was trimmed. He looked a typical farm boy, and as we went to get him, he blurted out "Please, sirs, not this! I'm a southerner too, sir. I ought not to be slave, sirs, so please don't brand me - my folks live in Arkansas, and although they're only poor farmers, I'm sure they could scrape together enough to buy me from you, sirs, an release me back to our family."

I was a bit startled by this, and thought he must be lying, and so I snapped "Rubbish! You're a northern soldier, who came and tried to invade us."

"It wasn't my fault, sir. I was in the marines, and my unit was stationed up north when the war began... So what could I do, sir? We were ordered to come down south when the war started...."

"You should have done the right thing, boy!", Jon cut in. "No real southerner would bear arms against his fellows. You should have deserted or something, and made your way back to your folks. Or rejoined the southern forces, properly."

"But my buddies, sir..."

"So where are your buddies now, to help you? No, boy, you brought this on yourself by denying your heritage. You're a slave now, and that's it. There's no going back, and I doubt that you'll ever see your folks or that Arkansas homestead again." Jon was really tough on things like that, and I suppose he's right - I mean, if you or I had been in New York or somewhere when the war finally erupted, we wouldn't have fought for the Yankees, would we, Stu? We'd have got back home and joined out forces, defending our right to the way of life the southern states have chosen. Mind you, it did make me feel a bit uneasy - I wondered how many other southern boys had been enslaved like this, as there were far more southerners in the old combined forces than northerners - all those Yankees work in offices and such, and the poor southerners have always traditionally ended up in the army as there was no other work. Still, that's one of the penalties of fighting a civil war, I suppose - there are always going to be some cases of unfairness, but it's pretty minor in relation to all the other things that went on.

He carried on shouting and arguing as Jon and I herded him over to the frame with our prods, and Jon showed me how important it is to have the slave tied absolutely immovable. If his body can even twitch a little, the edge of the brand won't be sharp and crisp, and it spoils the effect. We use an adaptation of the standard "flog and fuck" frame - the slave can be secured on his belly on the cross piece and his legs strapped rigidly to the back legs, and then you throw a strap around his waist and really haul it tight to make sure his butt can't move. There are additional straps that go around his thighs, too. It's the right arm that's the real problem - the left one is just cuffed to the front leg as usual, but there has to be a special platform to take the right arm straight out. Jon really tugged at the binding around the slave's wrist to keep his hand flat on the platform, and then it's really fiddly to tighten all the individual ones to hold the fingers down. Jon explained that it's pretty bad when the branding iron sears their butt, but there aren't all that many nerve endings per square inch down there. But on the back of the hand, it's different and it's so much more sensitive.

Actually, I'm glad we'd eaten lunch before the branding, as I'm not sure I'd have fancied it afterwards as it's pretty stomach-churning. I'd not been to one before, and I suppose that like a lot of people I was just aware of seeing the slave brands on the butt and hand, but hadn't really considered how they got there. There's an awful lot of noise, of course - all the slaves, without exception, scream as the branding iron goes into their flesh - and remember it has have to stay there for five or ten seconds, to sear through the outer layers of the skin, and all this time the slave's screaming is really pitiful. They tend not to stop, either when you put them in at the back of the "crush", and stand there sobbing for a couple of minutes. If you add in the shouting and pleading form the slaves still to be done, it's pretty wearing, I can tell you. You'd have thought that big tough soldiers would be more stoical, and would have seen that what was going to happen to them was inevitable, but it didn't stop all of them shouting all the time. But it's the smell that's the worst - not so much the smoke and smell of burning meat, as that's not all that different from a barbecue at home. No, it's the fact that most of the slaves lose control of their bowels and bladders, and there's soon the awful smell of shit everywhere. The big slave who's in charge of he brazier and the heating of the irons has to clean up the mess off the floor after each one, but it's still not very nice.

It's bad enough for the slaves, I suppose, but I have to tell you, Stu, that your old buddy Steve was pretty scared himself! Jon insisted that I actually do the branding personally, as it's another powerful way of reinforcing to the slaves that I'm in total control of them. I've never done anything even remotely like this before, and I was terrified of fucking it up and potentially ruining a valuable slave, especially as Jon went on and on about making sure I pressed the iron in with a firm, even pressure, about not being distracted by the slave, and by him telling me of the need to keep count of the time - as you first touch the iron to the skin you start saying to yourself one and two and three and four.... To make sure you leave it there long enough, but not too long. It's not so bad doing their butts, actually, as it's a nice big area, it's not so critical for timing and pressure, and at least you can't see the slave. But when you come to do the back of their hand, it's different - you have to get it lined up quite precisely, you have to make sure you don't press too hard as you don't want to risk destroying any of the nerves that control the fingers, but what's worse is that the slave is looking right at you. His head is there, just where you're trying to work, and he's screaming and shouting away with a terrible mixture of fear, pain, and downright hate for you.

You know, Stu, it was made worse by thinking about what that young Arkansas guy had told me. If the war hadn't finished, you and me might have been fighting, just like him. And the northerners could have captured us, and it could have been us strapped there on the frame, waiting to get our butts branded. But then, I suppose it wouldn't have been so bad for us, as the northerners don't have slaves, do they? That's what got this whole stupid civil war thing stated in the first place.

I was pretty upset, and not a little nauseous, by the time all nine had been done, and Jon said hat that was enough for one day: we still had some stuff to do the slaves, but they needed to be allowed to recover. So one by one we took them out of the "crush" and marched them over to the slave sheds, and locked them in to "their" cage. It's a lot of effort, when you need to escort them individually like this with your slave prod, and I'll be glad when they've finally become resigned to their status - Jon says it always does happen - and are no longer at risk of escaping, and just obey orders. Steve.

Steve: Frankly, it all sounds absolutely barbaric. How can you get involved with this? Stu.

Stu: Hey, it's not very nice to get these critical one-liners from my oldest buddy. Don't blame me, blame the system! Mind you, I didn't like branding the guys much as it really did hurt them, and over a beer last night I talked about my concerns to Jon. He made a number of points, that I think you ought to consider before criticising me!.

Firstly, it is the law. All slaves must be branded. No exceptions, no excuses, as I've told you. Dad's company has to use slaves to be competitive, and so we have to brand them. Or else we'll be fined.

Secondly, think about the consequences of not branding them - or, indeed, of not having slaves at all. Jon says that in all major wars in the past soldiers were ultimately repatriated to their homes. But that's when foreign soldiers come in and invade, and even then it's far from total: we and the British ultimately repatriated the Germans in WW II, but the Russians kept many of them for a long, long time. But it's different when it's a civil war - these guys aren't foreigners, who invaded the country, Stu. They're our own countrymen, who came down here and tried to change our way of life. What are we supposed to do with all the captured soldiers? We can't just send them back and let them go free, or the north would be tempted to do it all over again, so they've got to be kept down here in the south. So either they've got to stay in prison for the rest of their lives, which costs a huge amount to do, and which isn't very good for the guys anyway, or we have to adopt the solution we have: gradually sell them off as slaves, so that they cost society nothing and the men can lead useful and productive lives. Now, if these guys were "foreigners" who were enslaved, that might be OK as you can generally tell a foreigner from one of us because of their colour, or their slitty eyes, or something. But they're the same as us, Stu: we were all citizens of the same county, speaking the same language, used to the same laws and customs, and everything. So if you make a guy like that a slave, how are you going to be able to locate him amongst the rest of us if he escapes? Collars can be cut off, and the brand is the only sensible way of permanently identifying them.

And thirdly, Jon points out that it's best for the guys themselves. I know that sounds odd, but it's difficult for a free man, especially one brought up in a country like ours, to accept that he's now a slave. Stripping him and collaring him starts the process, but once you've burned a brand into his skin, the guy can be in no doubt about what he is. Stu says it's a kindness, really, to help them through this difficult transition as quickly as possible.

I'm not a complete monster, you know that - or, at least, I hope you do! That night, when they were all in their cage, I went along with a big jar of burn salve that Jon gave me - again, it's me that has to do this, as they're "my" men and they need to know that it's me who's looking after them. They have to be branded without anaesthetic, Jon says, as you want them to really remember their transition to full slavery, but there's no point in prolonging their suffering unnecessarily and so the burn salve was there to help. I must say the branding scars look pretty horrific at this stage as I smeared the antiseptic analgesic stuff on to them, and I didn't even get the expected "high" from getting to feel their butts! But Jon tells me they'll scab over very quickly, the when those drop off, the brands will be sharp and clear and not at all unpleasant to look at. He said I did a good job with the branding iron, and there's not many guys my age could have performed as well - I feel quite proud. Steve.

Steve: Look, stop making excuses, will you? You sound as if you've got it all worked out, but it's not right to take free men and turn them into something approaching animals! Do you realise that you've never even mentioned any of these nine men by name? You've already effectively dehumanised them. I'm not sure I want to hear any more about the horrible things you do to these poor unfortunate guys. And I think you should talk to your dad again about getting out of this whole mucky business, and coming to college here in Atlanta. It's fun, and I miss having my old buddy with me - the other guys in the dorm are all very serious and don't want to sneak out and try to bluff the bars into serving them a beer, and life would be a whole lot brighter if you and me could chase the tail together and do again some of that "good guy, bad guy" stuff that made us so successful at getting laid in High School. And are you certain that this _on is a good influence on you? He sounds pretty cold-blooded to me. Stu.

Stu: I hate to say this, but I think we're growing apart. They say that always happens when people go away to college: you lose touch with your buddies. You're there, going to classes, "chasing tail", living in the dorm (from what I hear, those places can be fun), fooling the barmen, and still living the kind of irresponsible life we used to when we were at High School. But I'm a working man, Stu, doing a responsible job. I've got other worries now, like making sure my slaves are properly trained, and convincing Jon that even though I'm young, I'm as capable of doing the work as the other draymen are. You probably can't understand how hard it is for "the boss's son" to be accepted as a genuine worker by his colleagues, either. I think you're just postponing "real life" by majoring in eighteenth century English poetry - if you were out in the real world, as I am, you'd begin to realise how hard it is to make a living these days with the economy still on its knees after the war - we ought all to be trying to do our best for the country, not idling away our time in some Elysian academic paradise. And, I'm beginning to think Jon's a pretty great guy in spite of what you said in your last note - he looks after my interests, advises me, and really knows "the world". I really admire him, and hope I'll be half as good one day as he is now. I must go now - I've got to be at the yard by six to get the slaves started. Think about what I said, buddy: I hope I can still call you that. Steve.

Steve: Hey, lighten up! Do you remember that story we studied in English class about the dictator who said he was fighting a war for "truth, beauty, poetry, and things like that". And then when it had been going on for years and years he asked for a poet to write a commemorative eulogy for one of his generals, and was told that there were no poets any more, as they'd all been drafted into the army to prosecute the war effort? Well, I think you're in danger of being just a little bit like that - sure, we need to rebuild after the war, and civil wars are particularly hard to recover from so history tells us. But there's no point in guys like you working away to "rebuild" unless there's something to "rebuild" - we need poets, just as much as we need slave drivers, Steve. But please let's not quarrel over this - I value our friendship, and I don't want to lose you as a friend, and I'd hate to miss out on our correspondence, even though I find some of it a bit - well - upsetting, shall we say, and leave it at that? And I'm still concerned that this Jon is too much of an influence on you. I guess the worst is over for your slaves anyway? Your buddy...(?) Stu.

Stu: Hey, just stop criticising me, OK? You do your thing and I'll do mine. Don't worry about Jon - he's a great guy, as I've said. I really enjoy working with him. And you are coming back home for the holidays, aren't you? I ought to have my team properly trained by then and you can come out for a ride on the dray with me. I thought it was all going well today - I got to feed the slaves myself for the first time, as it's another of those things the drayman does himself to bring him closer to the slaves. It's awkward until they're properly trained, though, and you can trust them to be out of the cage, as you have to do each one individually and it all takes time - you get the slave to kneel in front of you with his back straight and his butt resting on his heels and his hands clasped behind his back, then you press the spout of the feeder into his mouth and give one turn of the handle, and there it is!

The feeder is a special thing that I've not seen before - the slaves at home eat normal food, the scraps from the table, supplemented by slave chow. But the slaves here are fed a special very high protein low volume diet and you literally stuff it down their throats! As you turn the handle on the feeder the very small quantity of food paste goes directly from the feeder's spout down the slave's throat. Jon says this had two benefits - firstly, the slaves' teeth keep in good condition, as there's no sugar and stuff in the mouth to rot them, and you don't need to keep cleaning their teeth as there's no food lodged in the cracks or anything. But the very low volume concentrate has a major benefit in that the volume of crap the slaves produce is tiny, and it's hard and consolidated into one, or at the most two, tiny turds a day. This means that it's very unlikely the slaves will have a desperate desire to shit when they're working in the streets, and, if the timing is wrong and they absolutely have to, the very hard, small turd is relatively inoffensive, and can simply be rolled down into the nearest drain in the street.

I thought I'd got the hang of it, and was doing OK, when one of the slaves, as I let him out of the cage, tried to take the feeder himself and said something like "I'm not a goose, to be stuffed like that, as if you're making foie gras...". Jon was close by and slapped his face, hard, as that's simply outrageous behaviour for a slave, and the slave in turn swung a punch at Jon and almost felled him. It was fortunate that I had my slave prod to hand, and I was able to help Jon to his feet as the slave lay there writhing in front of us.

Jon looked grim. "Ah, well, at least it's happened early", he said, and we began preparations for what I thought would be the day's work by leading the other slaves off to the "crush" and imprisoning them there. The slave who had struck John and was still twitching on the floor from my prod (I'd had it set to the default of "maximum" as I hadn't been expecting to use it) and we hauled to his feet and secured him to a flogging horse that's always waiting there in the area - his legs were spread wide and you could see his big dick and balls hanging down between his thighs. Jon didn't bother with the waist and upper body cinch straps, just the ankle and wrist cuffs, as he said that for what we were about to do it would be more instructive for the other slaves to see this one as a "buckaroo" as he called it, when the slave's body is mostly free to move but where he's still unable to escape from the horse.

Jon went to the cupboard and came back with a strange instrument with a handle on the side that looked a bit like a pair of pliers - no, more like a chuck on an electric drill, as there were several pieces to the "head" - and a thick black ring made of rubber, with just a tiny hole down the middle. He went over and walked down the line of slaves standing there tightly jammed together in the "crush", showing them the ring, then slipped it over the drill chuck thing and turned the handle on the side of the instrument. Slowly, very slowly, very slowly indeed as the thick rubber of the ring needed a huge amount of effort to stretch it open, he continued to turn the handle until the jaws of the thing were right open and there was a large hole through the rubber ring, now stretched extremely tightly indeed.

He walked over to the helpless slave on the horse, knelt down, and began to "knead" the guy's balls, massaging and pushing them so that they were right down low in his sac. Then, as the slave almost groaned in pleasure from this, he slipped the sac down into the instrument, moved something that released the jaws, and the thick black rubber band snapped back to its "rest" position, but now firmly around the root of the slave's sac - we heard the "snap" of the rubber, but it was instantly drowned out by the slave's totally agonised screaming, It almost made me vomit, to think about the pain the guy must be in as the ring squeezed those delicate tendons and tubes in his sac, and I don't think I'd ever heard anything before quite so terrible as the howling from the guy - it just went on, and on.

Jon beckoned to me, and we went outside into the fresh, morning air, leaving behind the horror he'd just caused. I started to remonstrate with him, and he said quietly "Steve, you're not thinking! Look, why do you think we buy nine slaves when we only need eight? It always happens, one of them takes a shot at us, and we always do this."

"...but the slave's in agony", I blurted out, and he said "Yes, but only for a while. It only takes about an hour for the guy's balls to die, as that ring totally cuts off the blood supply."

"....but it's cruel...". He shook his head, as if in disbelief. "Look, Steve, you're not thinking like a drayman yet! You've got to control eight slaves, right? They've got to understand that they are slaves, and that if they disobey, the most terrible punishments are waiting for them. And you've got to control them on the open streets, where there are unlikely to be other guards and so on around. And they're not chained up when they're working, remember - they've got to load and unload the dray! How do you think you're going to do that? Well, I'll tell you - firstly, by being the acknowledged 'leader' of the pack of them - that's not as hard as you'd imagine, as they're all soldiers, and by their nature, soldiers tend to be the type of men who are predisposed to follow orders. But secondly by having them understand that you are ruthless - you'll prod them if necessary, order them to be whipped if they displease you, and you'll even be prepared to make them pay the ultimate sacrifice for a man, and take his balls."

"But even so...."

"No, Steve, it's best this way. One of them suffers, suffers terribly, I'll grant you that. But the other eight have learned a lesson they'll never forget, and it's kinder for them, in a way: this one demonstration of our power over them, done early, will save them from a whole load of trouble in the future, and if we hadn't done it, you'd have almost certainly have had to order a few whippings for them - and that's not pleasant, as making them work with whip scars and fresh blood, with the flies and all...."

Well, to cut a long story short, we left them for a couple of hours, and when we went back in the slave's balls had gone all black, and he'd stopped screaming and was now just whimpering, almost to himself. Actually, it was the slave I was most worried about - he'd got those kind of thick, "brutish" features that implied he was a real redneck, and he had a kind of swaggering insolence where his whole attitude was one of "I know best". I think he'd been some sort of corporal, and I could well imagine him terrorising the younger recruits in his platoon. In a way, I was glad he was gone, as I thought my task of controlling the other eight would be much easier now - so I could see that maybe what Jon had said was correct.

The other eight in the "crush" glared at Jon and me but didn't dare to say anything - they were beginning to learn that held tight in there they were very vulnerable to the lightest stroke of the prod, and it didn't just hurt one of them: the others, making close electrical contact because of their sweaty skins, caught it too. We called in slaves to take the eunuch away, and Jon told me, in a voice loud enough for my slaves to hear, that the ring was left on for a few more hours, but then the sack and dead testicles had to be cut off as otherwise there was a danger of gangrene setting in. "He'll end up as some lady's servant, probably", he went on. "As you take this crop of fine male slaves on your delivery runs, you might even see him, trotting behind some lady as she goes shopping, carrying her packages, her umbrella... All that sort of stuff. It's quite the fashion now to have a gelding performing these little services for fashionable ladies."

We really had to press on then with the remaining parts of the slaves' "processing" - firstly, one by one, they were taken out of the "crush" and fitted with permanent cock rings - well, not the sort of recreational ones that guys like to wear sometimes, but proper "working" ones. The rings are so tight that there's no way you can get the dick and balls through them, even when the slave's not erect, so the blacksmith fits them - there's a special shaped pliers that squeezes an open ring tightly closed and the ends are glued together: Jon says that it's not so long ago that they had to be welded shut, and that was a big problem as there's just no way you could stop the slave's body and balls getting burned at the same time, so we do seem to be making progress in dealing with these guys humanely - that ought to please you. And finally, long after it was our normal lunch time, we had the tattooer in to ink them.

They're required by law to have their SIN tattooed under their armpit of course, as are all slaves, but in the Company we also have it done as a barcode on their right biceps as it makes it easy to use modern technology to scan them when we're doing inventory and so on.

Jon whispered to me that it's also good as yet another means of reminding the slaves that they're just property now, and accounted for just as we do for any other items on the company's asset register. And finally, just as they thought they were finished, we took them all out again and one by one we had their backs inked. I'd read their files by now - we got them from the Department Of Defence as part of the war settlement, so I knew their names - and thought that we'd just use shortened forms of these on them: Dan instead of Daniel, and so on. But it just shows you what a good man Jon is, as he counselled me to only have numbers on them: the big digits 1 to 8, running from their necks to just above the start of their butt cracks. "If you let them use their names, Steve, it seems as if they're almost like men, whereas a number reminds them that they're just 'things' now. Some guys like their slaves to have 'pet' names and have them inked with 'slave' names like Binky and Snotty and so on, but I don't think that looks very professional - we are part of a major business here, and so I'd advise you just to go for numbers". So I did.

I was really peckish after all that, I can tell you, and was ready for lunch. But before Jon and I could eat we had to take them out, still individually, to the "exercisers" in the yard. They're like big treadmills that you find in the gym, except that they slope upwards so the slaves are always running slightly uphill as it's better exercise for them, and there's a big elastic harness you put on them that drags them backwards and which they have to work against. It looks pretty good exercise, actually - of course the slaves have to be cuffed to the side bars to prevent their escape, but once you've done that, you can just leave them: you set the timer and speed control for the amount you want to exercise them, and that's it. The spiked bar at the back means that they can't stop, or else it's pretty painful for them! Jon says my slaves are still in pretty good shape as they were in a holding camp that made them exercise, and it ought to be only a week or so before they've re-build enough muscle to be able to get them to work properly. This slave stuff is really interesting, the more you get in to it. Steve.

Steve: I know you said "stop criticising me", but, old buddy, don't you think it really is cruel to be treating the slaves like this? They are men, after all! And castrating that one, even if he was a swaggering bully... I'm not sure I can go on writing to you. Stu.

Stu: You know nothing! You just don't understand, do you? These aren't men, they're slaves. The sooner they acknowledge that, the sooner they understand that they've got a different life now, the better it is for them. And none of the things we did are really cruel - castrating that one did I'm sure make it a whole lot easier for the others. And the cock rings are a big help - if you are going to live and work totally naked, imagine how you'd always be worried about catching your dick and balls in things, or even sitting down "wrong" : the rings keep them all up and more out of the way. And I do need to be able to command the slaves, so I have to be able to distinguish them and what easier way for a naked body than by a big number that's clearly visible? And I'm sure it is kinder to do that than to keep reminding them of their former lives by using their names. I think you'd better shut the fuck up about things you know jack shit about - your dad won't even have domestic slaves, after all, so perhaps you just don't understand anything at all about the slave mentality and how he needs to be made to work. Steve.

Stu: OK, I did put the phone down on you. But you sounded so fucking self-righteous when you rang me after my long note, when we hadn't corresponded for a week as we were both so pissed off. Look, I miss you, Stu, as I need someone to talk to - all the other guys here are much older, as they say you can't be tough enough to be a good drayman until you're thirty or so, and I come in from a fair amount of joshing from them. I reckon it's a test dad's putting me through. And it's worrying enough, trying to handle all these big slaves and making sure I'm doing the right thing, without having to go around worrying about what my oldest buddy thinks. So let's just agree to differ on this, shall we? I'll tell you how I'm getting on, and you can tell me about college life, and when you come home for the holidays we'll really sort it out - I'll take you for a ride on my dray (I ought to be properly in control by then).... And I'll show you one or two other things I've learned, old buddy.... Jerking off isn't the only thing that two buddies can do together! OK? Steve.

Steve: Look, you'll never convince me that owning slaves is right. But we've been buddies for so long, it would be stupid to break up over it. It was so good to hear form you again, Steve - and what's all this about "what we can do together"? Stu.

A Boner Book

38

PART 3

Stu: Look, all that time we were jerking each other off after school we were losing out big time! There's a few things Jon knows that I wish someone had told me earlier! When we'd got the slaves locked up after their first afternoon of proper exercise - that same afternoon we'd gelded the ninth slave - they were all pretty dead beat and they didn't cause any trouble, probably because they knew that we could take their balls, too. Jon said that over night they'd have time to think about what they'd seen, and the next morning they'd be much more respectful of me. I was feeling pretty miserable, though, as it had all happened so quickly - the slave trying to take the feeder, the slap from Jon, and then me needing to "prod" him... And then the inevitability of the gelding - I felt it was somehow "my fault" as if I'd been less hesitant about stuffing the feeding tube into his mouth, the slave might not have reacted as he did and would still be a proper man. I know that's stupid, as the slave was totally at fault for not accepting being fed, and then for hitting out at Jon, but I still felt bad. And it was raining, too, and I knew I had to walk five blocks to the street car as I no longer brought my trap to the depot. All in all, I was feeling pretty miserable.

Jon saw I was kind of "slumped" when they were at last all locked away, and put his arm around my shoulders and said "It's tough at first, Steve, but you're doing OK, son. I've trained lots of draymen, and some of the older guys who've mostly been in the forces and got to the rank of sergeant didn't take to it as well as you are doing. Come on, let's go and have a drink with some of the other guys." Well, I was kind of worried about that as they're pretty strict in our town on underage drinking, as you know, and I thought we'd be in for problems as Jon led me in to the bar across the street from the depot, where all the draymen and other workers in the depot drank. I should have told you, though, that during the afternoon my uniform had arrived - the company likes all its draymen to have a proper "public face" so we have a uniform of dark khaki short sleeved shirt, matching shorts, and those tan "work" boots with the thick rubber soles. I'd also got my "accessory" belt, too - a thick leather one, which has fastenings to carry my cell, the radio-linked "panic" button I can press in an emergency (although Jon says none of the draymen has ever done that as they would never want anyone else to know they had a situation they couldn't deal with), my slave prod, the tawse, and, at the side, rather like one of those ceremonial swords you see soldiers wearing in formal uniforms, a short holster for the punishment cane.

Mind you, I was a bit embarrassed by it at first as the shorts are cut very short - you know how the fashion is now, for free men's shorts to come below the knee, but these stopped only an inch or two below my crotch! I thought there had been a mistake, and I did look a bit funny with my tanned calves but then the white bit where my normal shorts covered my thighs, but Jon explained that they were like that to make it easier for me to work in the rain, and that I'd find that out as soon as it happened. He also told me that draymen didn't wear underwear - and pointed out that the leg line of my briefs was showing through as the shorts are cut tight around the butt. I know we quite often used to go commando in jeans and stuff, but when I went and took off my briefs in the men's room, it did feel strange to be walking around in these tiny shorts with only the tightness of their legs against my thigh holding my dick and balls in.

As we went through the door into the bar I was hit by the smell of the beer and that special exciting "something" that says this was overwhelmingly a place where real men gathered. A lot of the other draymen looked up as we came in, and when they saw me in my new uniform they all cheered, to welcome me, and at once a bottle of beer was thrust into my hands. Jon and I joined a group of them and we talked about all the stuff guys talk about, and I had another beer bought for me. And then it was my turn to buy a round, so I went up to the bar and, with some trepidation, ordered.

The bar tender was a free man, and he just looked at me and said "We don't serve kids in here!", and the next minute he was lying half across the bar as one of the other craymen, a huge guy called Matt, had just reached over, grabbed his shirt and pulled him towards us, right off his feet! "Hey, fucker", Matt snapped, "This here's a drayman, not a kid! He's old enough to work a dray with slaves, and so he's sure as fuck old enough to drink in your bar!". The bar tender tried to say something about it being against the law, and this huge Matt said again "Perhaps you didn't hear me.... You serve a drayman, whatever he orders, or else I'll drag you outside and beat the shit out of you.... I was in the marines...." He let go of the bar tender then and stood there with his big beefy hands, looking very threatening, and the bar tender stood there, and then went and fetched my beers. "Thanks", I said to Matt. "Hey, kid, it's not for you I did it - but in the Corps we learned never to let civilians talk the service down... And it's the same here: these guys who do these jobs like tending bar need to know that they are here to serve real men like us doing real jobs, taking real responsibility for the lives of the slaves." I hadn't thought of it like that, but I could see that in our uniforms, there could be a certain esprit de corps, so I thanked Matt, and bought him a beer. There's a certain thrill in doing something illegal, isn't there?

Well, by about nine I'd had a few, and it was way past the time when I was expected home and I began to worry that dad would be cross

- you know how he is, always worrying that as his son I might be a tempting kidnap target. I wanted to call him, but my speech was a bit slurred, and when Jon saw the problem he used his cell to call dad instead. I heard him say that there'd been a bit of trouble with my slaves, and so he, Jon, had advised me to stay on and "settle" them properly that night, and as it would be very late, it would probably be better for me to stay over in the BDQ" (that's the Bachelor Draymen's Quarters - the place where Jon had his rooms, and the other small apartments where some of the other guys lived, in the depot).

We had another couple of beers, and Jon almost had to help me back across the road into the depot! He said I should stay in his apartment, and it's quite a nice place - a bit austere, as you'd expect for a single guy who's been in the forces - just a living room with a kitchen area in one corner, a bedroom, and a bathroom opening off the bedroom. He rummaged around in the cupboards and produced a sheet, blanket and pillow and told me I could sleep on the couch, then went through the bedroom and into the bathroom, and I could hear him pissing and cleaning his teeth. I messed around kind of arranging the stuff on his couch, then when I'd heard that he'd done, went through into the bathroom - by this time he was in bed, and for the first time I could see his naked torso as he lay there, the sheet pushed down to his waist. He'd got a bit thatch of black hair, shading a little to grey, and he just lay there with his arms up as he had his hands clasped behind his head in that really relaxed way that confident guys have (nice hairy pits, too!). I felt all kind of smelly and dirty after being in the bar, and thought that a shower would be a good idea (it might also help to stop my head spinning a bit), so I turned on the water and stood in there quite a time. I thought about jerking off, as I'm always horny at night, but I don't much like doing it in the shower and it was only as I was drying myself that I realised that if I did it lying on the couch, Jon might hear through the door! But it was too late to do anything about it, and as I had no underwear or anything and didn't think I ought to sleep in my uniform shorts (which were really tight, as I've said), I just wrapped a towel around my waist - well, almost, as Jon only seemed to have small towels, and there was a big area of my thigh exposed.

I walked back out into his bedroom and he was still lying there, looking at me. I felt my dick start to rise, as he's a really handsome guy and the thought of standing there, almost naked, seeing him bare from the waist up, was a real turn on. I guess he noticed it, as he said quietly "That couch isn't all that comfortable - this is a big wide bed: you could bunk down in here with me, if you like." I was going to say no, as I'd only got this small towel to sleep in, when he reached out and tugged at it! It fell away, of course, as it wasn't very secure in the first place, and there I was, stark naked in front of him. My half-hard dick at once betrayed me, and shot to a full erection. I started to stammer something, but with his other hand he pulled the sheet aside to clear a space in the bed for me, and half wanting to, half not wanting to, I cautiously got in.

"You're not afraid, are you, Steve?", he asked as I lay there, right on the edge of the bed, and I told him that of course I wasn't afraid. "It's just that a kid of eighteen like you... well, you don't know how guys react to each other in situations like this. It happened all the time in the marines, with new recruits: they just didn't know how to behave when they first bunked down with their older buddies. But you're doing OK so far, Steve, so don't worry.... It was considerate to shower like that, and I could see you were interested so I helped you along a bit by taking that silly towel off - real men coming out of the showers just drape it across their shoulder... And then I saw you were very interested, very interested indeed. So don't be shy..."

As he said this, Jon's big hairy arm snaked out and kind of pulled me closer to the centre of the bed, closer to him. His legs intertwined with mine, and I could feel the heat from his body all along the length of mine. My dick almost shot its load there and then as it pushed against the hairy soft hardness of his belly. "There, that's better. The first thing you've got to learn, Steve, is that if two guys are going to bunk together they may as well get comfortable right from the start - we could spend all night pussyfooting around on the edges of the bed, and never get really comfortable, and then not get a good night's sleep. So it's better to get really comfortable, like this. Are you OK?"

I was more than OK, actually - I'd never been this close to another guy before, not even you, Stu. I mean, when we jerked each other off we just did it sitting on that couch in your folks' den, but now here I was, so close to this fantastic guy that I could smell his body, slide against him as we were both a bit sweaty, and my skin was almost tingling as I brushed against his furry chest and thighs. I almost gasped as I told him I was OK, as it was difficult to keep my voice normal as I was so excited. "There's another thing, Steve", he went on casually, as if it was the most natural thing in the world. "When two buddies bunk together, there's a potential difficulty with them sleeping as they're so aroused - especially for young, horny guys like you. I guess you normally jerk off before you go to sleep, don't you? Well, if you don't do that, you'll be thrashing around all night and that will mean that you won't sleep properly, and you'll thrash around some more, and then I won't sleep properly, either. So it's best if you jerk off now, and get it over with, OK?"

I wanted to say no, as I was a bit embarrassed, to tell you the truth; but the scent of him, the closeness, and the fact that I really was in difficulty as my dick was rock hard and aching with that ache you get when it's been erect as much as it can be for a few minutes and it's really straining and begging for relief, made it impossible to speak. He didn't wait, though, and still holding me close to him so that I couldn't move away (not that I wanted to), he reached down and began to fondle my dick and my balls. I moaned quietly, as it was so erotic - the warm body, the feeling of his hands playing with me.... And then it got better: the arm that was around my back moved down, and as he continued to gently stroke my dick, I felt his finger pushing gently at my butt... I know I moved my legs as if to welcome him, and then he was scratching at my pucker - no, that's the wrong word - he was playing with my pucker, kind of, and I was so on edge that I thought I'd blow my load there and then. He whispered "OK?", and I could hardly reply as it was the most amazing thing that had ever happened to me, and I could feel his finger now pushing into me. It was thrilling, exciting, and at the same time somehow "wrong", but so "wrong" it just had to be "right", so totally right to have this man want to use me like this.

Look, I'd never really had a guy touch my prostate before - I know we learned about it in biology, but there's a difference between seeing that funny-looking thing on those diagrams in the books (well, I mean, a dick doesn't even look like a dick in the diagrams, does it?) and actually having a guy, a strong, masculine guy, put his finger inside you and massage it as you're lying together. It was too much. I gave a moan, then a little cry, and my dick shot convulsively, and carried on shooting.... You know how it is, sometimes, those "after shocks" just go on and on an on. I could smell my cum as the warm air wafted up out from between our bodies under the covers and hit my nose, and I started to blush as I knew my cum must be all over his belly and chest. But he didn't seem to care - he just pulled me closer to him, and I was aware of his face so close to mine, with a big, happy grin all over it. "Wow!", he said. "I could tell you were horny when you came out of the bathroom, but that load you've just shot...." I started to stammer to say I was sorry, but he silenced me with a little squeeze and carried on "Hey, son, don't ever apologise for shooting a big load! As you get older you'll start to regret that you can't do it like that...."

His hand slid between us as he was saying this and I could feel it rubbing over me, all slippery, as it got covered in my cum. "Now it's my turn, Steve.... You OK with that?" He asked quietly, and of course I said yes, as I thought he was just going to jerk himself off. But instead, he moved his hand again and now his cum-slimed finger was going into me again, and again, and as if my body knew what it needed to do, I moved my legs slightly to make it easier for him. He didn't just push his finger up and massage me as he had before, though, but started to slide it in and out, and move it around, as if he was opening me up. I moaned and whimpered with the sheer excitement and pleasure of it - and then winced slightly as a second finger joined the first. He kind of "shushed" me and whispered "It's OK, Steve....", and soon I was moaning again as his skilled fingers stretched and excited my ass in a way I'd only dreamed about before. Look, Stu, we'd read all that stuff on the internet, but until you actually feel a guy playing with your ass you can't really imagine how great it feels - at one level it sort of hurts, but at another you're so overwhelmed by the excitement it's causing that you don't care.

I don't know how long it went on for, but after a bit, he stopped, moved his face away from me a bit, and looked hard at me. "You OK, son? Shall I go on?" Well I wasn't just OK, I felt fantastic! And I thought he meant was it OK for him to start to jerk himself off now, so I nodded and smiled, and smoothly, gently, using his strong hard body so effortlessly that it seemed so right, so natural, he pulled away from me, rolled me over onto my back, pushed my legs apart and knelt there between them, his dick jutting out over me. He put his hands above my shoulders and lowered himself down on me so that his dick almost got crushed against me, and plunged his face by the side of mine. I almost shot again as he nibbled at my ear lobe, and his hot, wet tongue plunged in and out of my ear, then he stopped, and now very, very quietly indeed, as we were so intimately close, again said "OK?"

I was so excited, feeling his body above mine, his dick pushing into my belly, that I couldn't answer properly, and just gave a totally satisfied murmur of assent. Somewhat to my surprise he pulled himself away from me so he was again kneeling upright, and then his hands were around my ankles, lifting my legs into the air and pushing my feet back towards my head. I was so surprised that I didn't at first know what to say - I mean, one part of me knew what was happening from those videos we'd watched together, and didn't want him to fuck me. But another part of me was excited and really turned on by this guy who was so clearly in charge and knew what he was doing. And another part of me knew I ought to say no, but didn't like to admit that it was my fault - I should have stopped him before, I shouldn't have jerked off, I shouldn't have got into bed with him.... I mean, you don't want to be thought of as a "teaser", do you, leading a guy on like that? And after all that propaganda they fed us in those fatuous sex-ed classes, I was worried that he hadn't even opened a condom, let alone tried to put one on. But even as I was thinking all that it was too late - I could feel his dick pushing at my hole!

Look, Stu, you and I never went anything like that far, did we? And I wish we had, now. Because it's totally amazing, utterly fantastic: I was looking up at him and his shit-happy smile had changed to one of grim concentration now as he pushed and pushed, to force his dick into me. "Push out! Pretend you're going to crap!", he snapped at me, and I was so confused for a moment that I forgot about the excitement of his hot dick head in such intimate contact with me... And that caused me to relax a bit, and he was in. I cried out, as it's painful at first even when you're all lubed up with your own cum and you've been stretched by this fingers, and he stopped for a moment, still looking down at me, and now with the faint trace of a smile starting to turn up the corners of his mouth. As he continued to look at me, slowly and deliberately he moved his hips forward and his dick slid up into me, and I cried out again, at first in pain, and then with joy, pleasure, laughter..... Look, Stu, until you've taken dick you just can't imagine what it's like: it's just the most indescribable feeling that goes through all your nerves, and makes you want to shout out, to cry, to laugh, to thrash your body around in total abandon... It makes you want to let go, to forget that you're Steve, a young guy who's never had proper sex, and you want to join in, to share, to suck his dick in and let it become part of you, to totally meld with the big, strong body that's towering above you, dominating you.

He fucked and fucked and fucked, and I was almost delirious with the joy of it. I knew my hands were reaching out for him and then running in ecstasy up his hairy thighs and grabbing at his muscular butt. I know my head was turning from side to side on the bed, and banging up and down. I could hear myself crying out "Yes, yes, fuck me, Jon..." And other disconnected strings of words like that. I could feel tears flowing down my face, tears from the pain, and from the ecstasy. Sweat was pouring off me. I could hear my breath rasping. I could feel the blood racing through me. And then it was over. I saw his whole muscular body arch backwards and his pubic bone slammed into me one last time, causing me to shout out again, and the most incredible look came over his face as his eyes screwed up and his mouth opened and he roared "OH yesss.....".

I knew he'd cum, and the next moment he leaned forward onto me again, taking most of the weight on his elbows. His face was next to mine, and he was grinning now, looking almost insanely happy. We were both soaked in sweat, and it was as if we might slide over each other. My body knew what to do - the moment he let got of my legs, I wrapped them around his waist and tightened them, as if I was trying not just to hold him inside me, but to pull him even further in! I could feel his heart racing and his lungs heaving as his body was pressed into mine. "OK?", he asked again, and at first I couldn't answer as I was laughing, crying, almost delirious with happiness. But then I managed to compose myself a bit, and murmured "Oh, yes.....".

We lay there for a couple of minutes, then slowly he pulled out of me and slid down beside me, putting his big strong arm around me again to continue to hold us close. "That was the first time for you, wasn't it, Steve?". I felt embarrassed to tell him it was, as no guy likes to admit that he's not experienced sexually, does he? But when I nodded, he went on quietly "I thought so.... But that's good.... You'd have looked pretty foolish when you started on your crew, if you didn't know what it as about."

The casual way he said that surprised me a bit, and I didn't understand what he was going on about. So I rested my hand on his pec, feeling his nip hard, stabbing into my palm, and asked him what he meant. "Look, Steve, you're a drayman, OK? You're a young drayman, sure, and we usually only have older, very experienced guys who can properly control the slaves. I was worried that you didn't really know what it was all about - but I think you'll soon be able to pick it up: you like sex, don't you?"

I thought that was a bit of a funny think to say, and so asked him if all young guys didn't like sex! "Oh yes, Steve - but it's different for draymen. You see it's another way we control the slaves, or, rather, turn them from being men who think they have free will, into totally compliant, totally obedient animals, pulling the dray and delivering the goods properly." He moved his body again, getting more comfortable as he warmed to his theory, and went on "Look, we've taken these men, who were all tough, virile, fighters, and we've stripped them, collared them, inked them, trimmed their pubes, and branded them. The point of all of this is two fold - firstly, there are the practical considerations, like collaring them and branding them marks them properly as slaves; trimming their pubes helps to make it easier to keep them clean, stops lice an stuff like that, and makes it cooler for them to work in the sultry heat we get down here. But the other reason we do all this is to teach them that they're no longer men, no longer in control of their lives, to the extent that we can do things like this to them and there's not a thing they can do about it. They're learning that their bodies are now under our control totally, and that's what we need: remember, out in the streets these slaves aren't even chained to the dray, as they have to be capable of delivering the packages and stuff. So if you have eight of these big, tough slaves under your control, it's only going to work if they fully accept that they are slaves, and you're their master. They have to accept that you're totally in control, that you give the orders, and that they obey, obey you totally and completely, that they can't even think of doing anything else."

His hand had crept to my nip now, and was toying with it, causing small shivers of excitement to flow through me again. "There's one other thing that we need to do, therefore, so that they totally accept you as their master and controller, and that's to get you to be in charge of their sexuality. Remember, these men, as they still think of themselves, deep down, are all tough studs who are married, and most of them have kids - we can research that in their files. But they were all in top-line units, which implies they've been in the service for a few years, and the pressure is on for those guys to get married, to produce kids, and show their buddies that they're 'real men'. A lot of them would probably like sex with their buddies, as they wouldn't have chosen that career in the first place if they weren't easy with being so close to a whole lot of other guys and being prepared to trust them with their lives. But it's not the done thing in the service to say that, and your buddies would laugh at you and call you a fag if you didn't go out and fuck women when you have a night's pass, and then if you didn't find some woman in your home town and get her pregnant. So they tend to see themselves as 'men' because they fuck women and sire kids, and part of their retraining as slaves is therefore to fuck them, fuck them hard, and fuck them often, so that they understand that they're now the subservient ones. Instead of being in control of these women, you're now in control of them; it's not their dicks doing the fucking, it's yours; and it's their wives' cunts, but their own asses that are taking it."

I was astonished, I can tell you! I mean, I'd wondered why they'd chosen such perfect specimens of manhood as dray slaves, as it would surely have been easier to use slightly less perfect guys, weaker ones (after all, on modern ball-bearing wheels, it doesn't require all that much effort to pull a dray - well, not until you get to the hills, I suppose.) - but now I could see it! These were the toughest, most virile ones the could find so that when they were forced to take dick they would crack and fail - it's like the difference between a piece of metal and a piece of glass, I guess: both are strong, but you can bend and twist metal quite a lot and it just "gives" and kind of goes with the flow, and you have to do a real lot of stuff to it before it fails. And glass is tough, too - look at all those glass protective panels on staircases and so on, and the windows in tall buildings that people can lean against without falling into the street. But when glass fails, it fails suddenly, and catastrophically. That's how our slaves were going to be - they would not bend and twist and put up with being fucked, but would break into a thousand pieces, and would then be easy to manage and control. Of course that's the psychological theory - I later found out that most of the draymen chose big, tough, muscled slaves as they're a whole lot more fun to fuck anyway. I mean, it's one thing to have a weak, thin guy under you as you fuck the insides out of him, but there's a whole lot more satisfaction in totally dominating and controlling the sort of body that could beat you to a pulp if it tried!

"You mean, I'm going to have to fuck all those eight slaves?", I asked. And Jon just gave me one of those big, lazy smiles of his. "Oh, Steve, I don't think there's going to be much of a 'have to' about it at all - I've been watching you, you know, and you like men, like them very much,

I think. So I don't think it will be any hardship for you at all to have to fuck your guys. I was a bit worried that you might not admit to yourself that you'd enjoy it - but after that little session just now I've got no concerns at all: I think that once you've learned how to use that dick you'll be a natural and those slaves won't get any rest at all. I take it you've not fucked a guy before?"

I blushed slightly as I said that I hadn't - I mean, a guy doesn't want to tell another one that he's not had sex, does he.... Especially at eighteen? I wondered if Jon was wondering what I'd been doing since I was sixteen, so I muttered "Well, not fucked, as such.... But I have been with other guys...." Stu, he just laughed! Not maliciously, or anything, but as if I'd told a great joke. "OK, Steve", he said "You've not fucked 'as such' - does that mean that you've bored a hole in a big juicy melon and fucked that? Or that you've just not gone all the way with a buddy before? I mean, they told me you're eighteen, and a horny, good-looking guy like you can't have been lacking opportunities...." So I told him about how dad tended to keep a tight reign on me, and how you, Stu, my best buddy, had those funny Christian parents who had kept telling you that sex was wrong - let alone sex with other guys - and so we'd only got to just fooling around with each other, and had jerked each other off and so on, but hadn't actually fucked.

He nodded, and it wasn't censorious or judgmental in any way. "Well I suppose that's good, as far as it goes", he went on, reaching down and stroking my balls a bit. "I can teach you how to do it properly, son. The first time you fuck a guy it will be great, right from the outset. So many guys experiment with real man-to-man sex and because they've not had proper lessons about it at school they make a mess of it and just don't enjoy it as much as they should. You may have been waiting for it, Steve, but now it's here, it's going to be great. We'll start in on those slaves of yours tomorrow."

I could feel my dick almost shrinking at the thought of having to force myself into one of those big, muscular asses, and he sensed this and smiled again. "First, though, we have to take control of them sexually in other ways.", he told me. "They know they're totally reliant on you for food and water, and now we're going to the next stage and they'll learn that you're in charge of them sexually, too. Tomorrow morning we tell them that from now on, even if they only want to jerk themselves off, they have to ask your permission."

"So if I'm going to fuck all these guys, I'd better go out tomorrow and buy some condoms", I muttered, which was a bit of an odd thing to say, I suppose, but we'd had all that drilled into us, hadn't we? "Steve, get real, will you! These are all breeders, Steve, who've been giving it to their wives and haven't had any chance to stray, not even with their buddies! You don't even want to think bout using condoms with these guys - it takes away all the pleasure. I certainly never use them, as even with the thinnest ones you immediately lose most of the sensation of your dick in direct contact with him, and you don't get the full warmth, the smoothness.... But most of all, Steve, it's putting a barrier between you and the other guy, at a time when you want to be completely open." Condoms are only for those who are scared about life, Steve - real men want to feel the other guys in intimate contact with them." With that he hugged me again and reached out and turned off the lamp, and I knew we were meant to sleep. But it's not that easy - although Jon was soon away, his breathing slowed and his whole body relaxed, I just couldn't. It was so exciting, being next to a guy in bed like that, having another man so totally close to me. I did sleep eventually, of course, but I need my eight hours and I certainly didn't get it, so when he slapped me on the butt to wake me up I did so with a complete start, and sprang up, wondering where I was! There was Jon, already dressed, looking down at me as I lay there - he'd pulled the covers off me and woken me like that, and now I realised that he was smiling as he looked down at my morning hard-on. "Ah, ready for those slaves already, Steve!", he said, "But get cleaned up, and well go over to the cafe for breakfast."

There were dome other draymen in the staff restaurant, and we joined them. I saw them looking at my somewhat dishevelled uniform, and my wet hair, and the way Jon was almost protective of me as we sat there and tucked into ham and eggs and toast and stuff, and I just knew that they all knew that Jon and I had been together all night. And I tell you, Stu, I didn't care!

I hope you sex life is progressing well, old buddy.... I'd hate to think of you just sitting there in front of our PC jerking off, all alone. Steve.

PART4

Steve: Hey, buddy, don't worry about me and my sex life. I'm getting on all right with Inga, the Scandinavian gir I told you about. And it's proper fucking, too - not up the ass! I'm starting to worry about you, Steve - are you sure you're not trying too hard at all of this? When you write about having to totally dominate and control those eight poor guys - yes, Steve, that's what they are, guys, just like you and me. And not, as you keep trying to tell me, "slaves". Slaves are men, Steve, men with feelings, needs, and as you mentioned, wives and families - I really get worried!

Look, I'm coming back home next weekend to introduce Inga to my parents. Please don't do anything foolish before then. Let's sit down and talk about it. Stu.

Stu: Hey, I know we've known each other for a long time, but I resent you telling me that I might "do something foolish". This is my job, Stu, and I have to do it well to prove to dad that I'm a capable, competent guy, not some high school kid filling shelves at the local market. And your fucking liberal shit all the time is starting to piss me off - they're slaves, Stu - S - L - A - V - E - S, not men. Jon told me that they forfeited their right to be treated as men on two counts: firstly, they came down here and invaded us, trampling over States' rights and everything, in defiance of the Constitution. They should have known that was wrong, and I don't care if they were just "obeying orders" which is the excuse some folk make for them - you aren't required to obey orders that cause a civil war and where you're fighting your fellow countrymen. And it's particularly bad for number four - that's what's inked on the big blond guy from Arkansas - as he might have actually had to invade his home town: even a big dumb Arkansas boy could surely see that was wrong. All that ought to be obvious to you, too, but Jon's second point isn't so clear unless you've been in the service too: these guys were all tough, hardened fighting troops - and they allowed themselves to be captured! I know some of the "actions", as they call them, were pretty bloody but that's no excuse - if they were fighting, they should have fought on to the end and not surrender and end up in a prison camp. A man who gives up like that forfeits any right to be treated like a man - he's a wimp, and he deserves to be ordered around by real men. So let's hear no more of it, OK?

I understand your family have always opposed slavery, and that's probably tainted you - but as I said in an earlier note, what else are we supposed to do with all these northern soldiers anyway? We can hardly send them "back" as it's our country, Stu - how could number four ever go back to Arkansas, when the last time he was going to be going there it was to rape and pillage and plunder? Surely even you can see that giving them good, healthy work, like on our drays, is better for them than to be kept confined in a prison camp for the rest of their lives? Anyway, we need the labour: with all the infrastructure they destroyed, it's going to cost billions and billions and take years to really get things back together properly. And whilst we're doing it, we may as well do it properly - put into place all that stuff they talked about for ages to protect the environment. It's really much better, you know, to deliver around town by a dray, rather than a gasoline truck - all that stopping and starting is bad for engines, and even with converters and everything they still pollute and use oil. But the biggest saving of all is that these guys aren't going to breed - that's really what's going to help save the planet. They've all got at least one kid already, and being the kind of men they are, I expect they'd all have ended up with at least two, if not three, or four - it's the kind of thing soldiers like to brag about, to prove how virile they are. They're never going back to their families, Stu and never going to be allowed to breed any more, and that's a huge saving for planet earth: at least eight, if not sixteen or even twenty four, fewer mouths to feed. And then you forget how much stuff these slaves would consume over their lifetime: automobiles, clothes, houses, fancy food grown all over the place, vacations, all that stuff: and instead of that, they'll just live simply in the barn here, and not use all those resources! Eight slaves in one small space, eating slave chow, just tread lightly on the earth, Stu.

Anyway, I must go: I've got to go and get them up, for another day's training. Steve.

Steve: As usual, you're trying to justify yourself. All this "ecology" rubbish - I didn't see you being so 'ecologically minded" at school. Come off it - I guess I have to accept that, rightly or wrongly, probably wrongly, slaves are a fact of life. But to have you spouting all this stuff to try and justify it, is ridiculous. Stu.

Stu: Ecological? Of course I was! It was you who came to school in that old gas guzzler that was all your folks would buy you. If you remember, I always came in my trap. And your folks use washers and dryers, and at our place the laundry is done by hand by the slaves. And in the summer they pull the big "punkah" things to provide a nice breeze, and we only turn the aircon on when it's really hot. Not using gas and electricity, Stu - that's real ecology.

Look, you're my oldest friend - I don't want this to come between us. Can we just agree to differ, and say that, as you point out, rightly or wrongly, we have slaves. You can say "wrongly" and I can say "rightly".

We can agree to differ on this, can't we, just as you actually believe in all that Jesus and god rubbish your dad spouts, whereas I lump it all together with the tooth fairy and Santa Claus? We used to debate that and we didn't really fall out over it, did we? So what's different about slaves? Look, if it makes you any happier, you can believe I'll be thrown down into the fiery furnace and burn for all eternity for my "sins", if it at least means that I can get a bit of peace right now, here on earth! Steve.

Steve: Oh, you always knew how to throw yourself about and argue to absurdity. It's probably what I like about you. I knew I'm not going to change your mind about this slavery stuff, any more than I ever managed to convince you about the love of Jesus (or, as you said, about the holy ghost, which you said ought to come out at Halloween!). So I'll just remember you in my prayers, and ask for mercy for you.... So let's move on. Tell me what happened next, then - in spite of being horrified by it, I'm curiously interested! Stu.

Stu: As long as you don't expect me to stand there silently as you and your family pray, you can pray for me all you like! That's more like it - the good old pragmatic Stu I know and love.

Well, where we? Oh yes, over breakfast Jon told me that it was time to start taking control of the slaves' sex, so when we'd finished we went over to the barn and shouted for them all to wake up. We were at the point now where I could "trust" them to be out of their sleeping cage all together, and I usually had them kneel in a long line in the way I've told you about as it makes going along with the feeder so much faster and easier. After I'd fed them I turned to them and before giving the order to allow them to get to their feet to go out to the exercise machines, I said to them "Right - do any of you want to jerk off?" They all looked vaguely shocked, and then looked at each other, and one or two mumbled "No, sir.". So I went on "This may be your last chance for some time. The rules are these: if you want to have sex, sex of any kind, with each other, or even with your own hands, you must in future ask my permission. You must ask my permission on each and every occasion you want to have sex - and, as I said, that includes jerking off. I will not always give that permission, especially on days when I have already offered you the chance to do it. For example, there will be no permission tonight, so that if you are in need of jerking off, you'd better do it now. If I ever find any of you have disobeyed this simple order an have had sex without permission, you will be punished, punished severely." You'd have thought that that would have been clear enough, wouldn't you - I've reproduced my words exactly as I said them, as far as I can tell. I mean, even the meanest intelligence would know that he wasn't allowed to jerk off that night now, wouldn't he? But even so, none of them wanted to jerk off then - they were all lined up still, and some of them were even semi-erect, so it would have been easy for them; but no, none of them did.

They were just on the exercise machines today, and as a further way of getting them used to my dominaton and control, I was careful to rub the sun oil into them myself - they've mostly still got white asses and so on from wearing shorts, even though most of their torsos are nicely tanned, and the exercise machines are placed so that for most of the day they're in full sunlight to help with getting them evenly coloured all over. We don't want them to come to harm, of course, as these are expensive assets, or even to be in pain or discomfort or else they can't proceed with the exercise programme, so we're careful to make sure they're liberally covered in sun protection. Up until today I've generally allowed them to rub it in to themselves, but Jon pointed out that having me do it would increase their sense of reliance on me, whilst at the same time giving me an opportunity of handling their bodies. He explained that a good drayman is always concerned about his slaves' general well being and good health, so it's not a bad idea to run your hands over them every day just to make sure there's no bruising, or sores, or anything like that. I'd already started doing this, running my finger around under their collars after morning feeding every day, and I know they appreciated this little attention from me as it enabled me to give them salve for the sores that inevitably form on the newly-collared until their skin toughens properly - these heavy metal collars do chafe, however carefully they're smoothed and fitted (and actually it's kind of sensual, running your finger in-between the tight collar and the slave's skin - you can feel his veins pumping, and the little movements of his Adam's apple as you go past it).

When they were lined up in front of the exercise machines, therefore, and had the big tub of sun cream open, they were expecting to be told to help themselves as previously. Instead, I took a big dollop on my hand, told the first slave to clasp his hands behind his neck, and began to rub it into his ass. You need to be thorough about something like this as the sun down here can be treacherous, especially towards noon, and so I needed to massage it quite deeply into the crack down his butt - but as my fingers slid down there, forcing his butt cheeks apart, the slave became restive and even dared to whisper "No, please.....". I had to give him a hard slap on the butt (and I'd forgotten that this hurts me as much as it hurts him - the bare palm on a good muscular butt isn't always a good idea!) and tell him to keep silent, but this seemed to do the trick - when I moved around and went to do his balls, he hardly made any complaint at all. It was good to feel his dick, too - there's something really nice about rubbing oil into a guy's dick, I think, and I was rewarded by him throwing a wood as I stroked him. I could tell he was embarrassed, though, as he almost shuffled his feet as I did this. The other slaves were watching, of course - although I'd told them to line up and assume "slave rest", I could see them watching me out of the corner of their eyes as they pretended to be looking to the front, and down - I made a note to correct that, of course, as a slave needs to obey at all times and not exercise free will like that.

I almost had problems with number two - he's the older one, the one who was a sergeant - when I came to do him. He was the first of the three un-cut slaves I have and he's very hairy - doing his butt had been difficult anyway, but when I'd done his dick and then went to skin him back, he did say "No, sir, it's OK....". Well, I had to slap him as a mark of displeasure for his speaking out of turn, of course, and my hand was already stinging so I didn't do it on his butt this time, but on his face. He looked really startled, and for a moment I thought he might even strike back, but fortunately for him (and for me - if he'd done it,

I'd have had to have had him gelded, and that would have been a real failure on my part) he managed to control his temper. So I went back and squeezed the end of his dick again to make his head pop out, and he shuffled his feet again and I sensed he was about to say something. I pre-empted this by saying "Easy, boy.... I'l just grease up your dick head so that if you spring a real boner today you won't get sunburn.... Think how painful that would be....." And gently massaged some of the cream into him. I could feel his body tensing as I ran my fingers over his dick head - un-cut guys are SO sensitive there, I find - and it was quite interesting for me, too to see how different in texture the head of an un-cut guys is: it's not just the fact that it's moist and shiny when it pops out, but the skin seems to be softer and finer somehow than on us cut guys.

It was true what Jon had said - after I'd finished them all, I did feel they were so much more "mine", and I know from their reactions that this unexpected attention from my hands on the parts of their bodies that previously they'd thought to be "private" had furthered their understanding that I was now totally in control of them. Mind you, it all takes time - massaging eight butts and eight dicks isn't something you can do in a couple of minutes, and it was eating into exercise time, time they needed to get their bodies back to that perfect state they'd been in as soldiers, before they were locked up in the internment camp. I know you go on about how it's not right that these soldiers had been made into slaves, Stu, but even you'll agree, I think, that having these men working for me, and exercising properly again, was better for them than being locked away in that miserable camp?

That evening I'd told dad I wasn't going home as I needed to observe the slaves, and so I ate with Jon and then he and I just lay on his bed generally just fooling around a bit, and talking. He really is a mine of information about the treatment and management of slaves, and I'm beginning to realise that dad was right not to let me go to college and insist I work here at the depot - a couple of hours with Jon, as well as being sexually exciting, teaches you more about slaves than any number of the lectures you'd get in the extra sessions now being added into all those "Personnel" and "Human Resources" modules. As

Jon says, most of those college professors have never actually driven a coffle of slaves, let alone had the guts to properly discipline them, and you can tell how unrealistic their view of the world is that they have made slave management part of "human resources" in liberal studies! He almost snorted as he said this, so clear is he that slaves are slaves, and not humans. Still, as we kissed and played with each others bodies, I did begin to wonder why he wouldn't let me fuck him, or even jerk off. But then, after a couple of hours, by about ten p.m., I found out.

Jon told me to dress and we went over to the security lodge, where Jon got the guard to re-play the surveillance tapes from the slave barn, and then to zoom down on to the cage with my slaves in it. We fast forwarded through it, watching them settle down into the straw after I'd left, and then shuffle and move around to get themselves as comfortable as possible for sleep - I've told you that the cages are deliberately on the small size, so that they only just have enough space and really can't avoid being in very close contact with their fellows, to increase "bonding" and to emphasise to them that things like "privacy" is not something that's now part of their lives. It was almost amusing, really, to see how, one by one, they managed to find a little bit more space, then half-turn over so they could jerk off and allow their cum to spurt directly down into the straw, rather than over the other slaves. "Apart form the fact that they're disobeying your direct order from this morning, they've got a lot to learn about proper bonding as a team", Jon commented. "These slaves ought at the very least to be jerking each other off - I mean, wouldn't you rather have even that minimal kind of sex with your buddies? But then, allowing the cum into the straw- it's pretty disgusting! I really don't understand why they all don't do what me and my buddies used to do in the service when we didn't want our sheets all stiff and hard - you can't use toilet tissue in the barracks, after all, or even a dirty T or your jock - you just catch it in your other hand, and lick it up. I guess most of them have been repressed as kids, and have been told that eating cum is somehow 'wrong'. Still, it looks as if most of them have jerked off -

and we don't want to have to punish them all as it will just take too long - so let's just make examples of a couple of them."

I decided that the ex-sergeant, number two, would be a sensible choice to be made an example of as the other slaves tended to follow his lead, and Jon, who volunteered his help, said that he quite fancied the young blond southerner, number four. We went over to the slave barn where we roused them all. I told them that we'd observed them jerking off against my express orders that morning, and that therefore they were to be punished, and unlocked the cage and made two and four come out. I made them drag two of the punishment horses over to where the others could see, and then ordered them bend over so that they were lying on the top plate, and fastened the straps to hold their wrists and ankles in position.

It's harder than you think to use a punishment cane properly - you need a proper swing, of course, to get your full power behind it. But you also want a fair degree of accuracy as you want each stroke to hit just an inch or so way from the previous one, as this maximises the pain for the slave and at the same time reduces the possibility of serious damage to the underlying tissue. It's fantastic, though, as you do it, as you see the big red mark across the skin come up almost as soon as you've struck. And you can tell the slave has been really hurt by the way that, even though he's securely strapped down, his body still tries to jerk forward as the blow lands, and the way he then vainly tries to shuffle around to give himself some slight easement, even though with secured ankles this is futile. There's the sound, too, of course - I did number two first, and the ex-sergeant tried as hard as he could to remain silent. My first stroke produced only a loud kind of grunt, but by the fourth on his butt he was screaming out in shock and desperation as it landed. I gave him six on the butt - three neat parallel lines on each cheek, as it's hard to get one stroke to cover both cheeks properly so I do each one separately - and then as a finale, I decided to give him two on each of his big thighs. This REALLY hurts - you probably can't imagine a cane stroke across the butt anyway, and to tell you the truth neither can I, except that I've seen the slave's reaction to it. But strokes on the back of the thigh are something else - two was really howling when I'd finished.

Sad to relate, that number four was a real wimp! I mean, he knew he was guilty as he'd been ordered not to jerk off, and had. But instead of taking his punishment properly, he lay there crying out and begging to be spared, as he was "a southerner, like us"! Well, I had to lay a stroke on him right there and then, before the punishment began properly, as I needed his full attention as I reminded him that he was no longer a proper southerner, and certainly not like us! He'd forfeited all those rights when he became part of the north's invasion army, and he was, I reminded him, a slave with no rights at all, except those I chose to give him. Then when I gave him the same strokes as I had to two, he screamed and sobbed and howled all the time.

We weren't finished with them yet, though, as Jon had advised me that I needed to reinforce these slaves' sense of being under my total dominance an control by using them sexually. So we left then strapped to the horses, and I stroked the palm of my hand gently over two's butt, feeling the warmth radiating from my handiwork. He tried to shuffle and move around as my hands explored his body, and as my finger probed down his butt crack he moaned gently "No, please, no....". But it was so exciting - feeling his warm moistness - and when my finger touched his pucker and his efforts to escape redoubled, it was just so dammed erotic that even if I hadn't been inclined to do so, I would now have pressed on anyway. I scratched gently at his hole, and he was murmuring "no, no, no...." all the time, and when I started to push my finger in, it got louder and louder.

To tell you the truth, Stu, I was all mixed up - I was really roused by the sight of two's big hairy muscular butt, but at the same time I was dead scared: I mean, I'd never actually fucked a guy before, and my only experience of it at all was having Jon fuck me! It was jolly good, really, that Jon and I had been together like this as at least I knew that it was going to be difficult - in some of those porn DVDs you see the guy's dick slam right into the ass, but that must be because the guy taking it is so used to it: for most of us you really have to work away trying to get your dick in, as even if it's really rigid, there's so much resistance that it bends and needs to be "coaxed". And, of course, I was a bit embarrassed! Not about the size of my dick, as you know I'm pretty well hung, but because I was going to have to drop my shorts in front of all those watching slaves and let them see me pumping away at two. Look, it's not as if I'm fat or anything, you know that - we always worked out together. But I'm kind of skinny, at least compared to those big strong muscular guys. And I'm so much younger than them, too - I think older guys, even guys in their early twenties, kind of look down on men of 18. And then there's always the risk of failure - suppose, by some terrible chance, I just lost my erection? Or if I didn't manage to cum?

Anyway, it needed to be done, and acting on Stu's advice, I went around to the front of two and dropped my shorts and just fingered my dick a little to get it properly hard, then asked him if he wanted to suck on it to lube it up with his spit. "Fuck you! I'm no cocksucker!", he snarled, and turned his head to one side, away from me. I deliberately didn't let myself get upset by this and instead of ordering further punishment for his insolence, I decided a little humiliation might work best, so I gently ran my fingers through his cropped hair as he lay helpless in front of me, and whispered "Well, two, 'fuck you' isn't a very nice thing to say to your master, especially when it's you who's going to get fucked!". With that, I went to go back to his ass, but it's not a very dignified thing to do with your shorts down around your ankles, and as I shuffled along I felt a real flush of embarrassment creeping its way up my neck at the thought of the slaves seeing me like that.

I soon discovered, too, that it's not a good idea to try to fuck a guy without any kind of lube or stretching, either! It's not that I was worried about hurting two, as he deserved it for the way he hadn't responded properly to me a moment ago. But it actually hurts you - without any lube, you just can't get your dick to even try to slide in past that sphincter, which anyway is clamped tight closed and trying to stop you from getting in. So I was embarrassed some more as I had to stand back and spit on my own hands to slime up my dick a bit before resuming my assault on him. And all the time he was bucking around and trying to get free, and shouting and cursing - I began to wish I'd tightened the belly strap on the horse so that he was more restrained, as being held there as a "buckaroo" made it even harder for me to force myself into him. At one point I thought I was going to fail dismally and that I just couldn't get my dick head in past his defences, and I began to really flush up with shame, and I could feel sweat soaking my uniform shirt and doing that kind of awful "cold trickling" down my ribs from my pits. I knew that if I failed on this I'd never make it as a drayman - if the slaves saw that I wasn't capable of taking two now, how on earth would I ever establish my proper authority over them? Once that thought had come to me, though, it was as if I was somehow possessed - I was determined that I wasn't going to have to go back to dad and tell him I'd flunked it - and my dick stiffened, and I just thrust on. I reached down and held my dick to stop it "buckling" in the middle, and then, almost miraculously, my dick head slipped in!

There was a most satisfying yell from two - I don't really know whether it was pain, or rage, or both, and, frankly, I didn't care. And now I knew I had him, as once in past his defences, there was absolutely nothing he could do to stop me going all the way. He was bucking around and twisting his body as best he could against the restraints, and somehow this only seemed to make it even more exciting for me, and, indeed, if he'd just lain there still and passive, it wouldn't have been half as much fun! I began to rock my hips backwards and forwards, pulling my dick in and out of him, at first slowly, and then with increasing vigour so that my body made a kind of "slapping" noise as it slammed into his. He was shouting out now almost in time with my action, and at the back of my mind I thought that at some point I'd need to discipline him sharply, as a slave ought not to use language like that about his master's actions - and I don't care if he was in the Marines, and that sort of language was perhaps common in the barracks room. I suddenly found myself enjoying it hugely - I'd forgotten all the anguish I'd gone through a few minutes ago, I didn't care if the slaves thought my butt was skinny compared to theirs (they saw it in action, forcing my dick in and out of their leader, after all, and that must count for something), and the sensations flowing through me were just indescribable. It wasn't only that exquisite feeling in my dick that always comes when you're in action, out the fact that my whole body was engaged in dominating, controlling and utterly subduing this big, tough, proud ex-marine. At eighteen, I was totally in control of a virile, strong male, a man who was completely unable to resist whatever I chose to do to him, however much he disliked it. It was all too much: so totally, amazingly, completely a turn-on, that very quickly - all too quickly, as far as I was concerned (but evidently not for the slave, who was still shouting and screaming) - I felt my balls begin to contract, and that fantastic sensation as my cum shot down my dick and deep up into the slave. I couldn't help it - it's almost automatic - I thrust myself really hard right into him one last time, my back arching as if it was determined to push my dick in as far as possible. And two's screams and shouts of protest were almost drowned out with my own cry of complete triumph.

Unfortunately I couldn't really enjoy the delicious "after sex" sensation - I'd have liked to throw my body along two's broad, sweaty back and just lie there, feeling him under me - but "duty" called and instead I pulled out of him, and stood up, looking over at the caged slaves who seemed almost frozen with shock at what had happened. One small advantage of feeding the slaves the low residue diet from the feeder is that their turds are small, and hard, and so the inside of two's ass was relatively clean, but even so I could smell that characteristic smell of shit drifting up to me from my dick, which was rapidly detumescing. Clutching at my shorts I went back to two's head and as he lay there, relatively immobile, and I wiped my dick through his hair to clean it a bit more. And then I pulled my shorts up and just stood there - two had stopped making all the dreadful noise now, and I grabbed his chin, sticking my fingers hard into the side of his face, to make him turn towards me. I was gratified to see that there were tears rolling down his cheeks, and these can't have been from the undoubted physical pain I'd caused him, as a strong ex-marine like that would never show such a sign of weakness. No, these were tears of shame, tears that signified that he was beginning to understand that he was no longer a free agent, no longer one who could swagger around with that supreme confidence that the physically powerful and beautiful have: he was a slave, and I was in total control of him. I stared at him, and said, loud enough so that everyone could hear, "You're a good fuck, boy! I'm looking forward to using your ass again, when the mood takes me." He remained silent, but I could see from the look in his eyes that I still had some way to go in properly taming him.

I enjoyed watching Jon fuck four then - he's the youngest of the slaves, the big blond "farm boy" from Alabama, who'd tried to tell me he was "one of us". Jon's a real cocksman, a true artist, and he fucked four with all the skill and determination that his long experience in controlling slaves had given him. Like two, four at first cried and shouted, but after about ten minutes he was just panting and moaning in rhythm with Jon's movements in and out of him.

When Jon had finished I undid the bindings holding two to the horse, and told him he could stand up. I was almost expecting trouble, and had my hand hovering over my prod, just in case, but two seemed somehow shattered, and just stood there trying to conceal the remains of his tears from the other slaves. I hope he appreciated that I gave him a couple of minutes to compose himself, before I opened the cage door and told him to enter. I did feel sorry for him, actually: there was a whiff of shit as he went past me from where I'd cleaned my dick on his cropped hair, and I knew he was going to be in for a tough time that night as he tried to find a space in the tiny cage without the others complaining - I could at least go back with Jon and shower properly - and that promised even more fun! Steve.

Steve: I can't believe it! You and that Jon raped two guys. And, what's more, you even sound proud of what you've done.

Stu: Don't be so fucking ridiculous! It can't have been rape - rape is what guys do to women, and other men. Try to get it in your head, Stu, that these are slaves. Let me spell it out to you again: S - L - A - V - E - S. You can't rape a slave, as he's not a woman, or a man! What we were doing was training two and four - training them to be good slaves. You have to understand that it's in their own best interests - until they properly accept that their lives have changed irrevocably, they aren't going to be happy and are always going to be fretting and worrying and trying to evade work and even to escape. And that would all be disastrous for them - at the very least, constant whipping, and for escaping, gelding or even death. It's kinder to get it all over with, to show them that they're just like animals, totally under their master's control - they'll be happy for it. Of course the fact that this aspect of the training is a huge turn on and a real fun thing for me to do is just a bonus!

I think you ought to remember the lines from that old Dylan song from last century that we both enjoyed when we were growing up... I can't get exactly how it goes, but wasn't there something in there about "....and don't criticise what you don't understand...."? I always liked that concept, and I think, Stu, if you and I are going to continue to be friends, that you'd better lay off making really rather unpleasant allegations about the way I'm treating these slaves. Let me remind you about the basic facts, old buddy: I've got to prove myself to dad. Therefore I want to be not just a good drayman, but the best drayman in the depot. Therefore I need a good set of dray slaves - no, not just good ones, but the best. And the only way you get good slaves is firstly to break them, and then to train them to your will. I've got no interest, no motivation, for treating them badly - far from it: I want them to think of me as a good master one they're glad to have, and one whom they obey implicitly as they know that I'm looking out for their interests, and am treating them right. A good master has the respect and trust of his slaves, Jon says - you can get obedient slaves just by repeated harsh physical punishment whenever they fail to obey; but if you want good slaves, slaves who go the extra mile for you, that only comes when they truly know you're the best master they're ever likely to have. There's just no percentage in it for me treating them badly!

So let's cut it out, shall we? I'll continue to write and tell you about my life, and you can tell me about your progress with Inga, your forays into the academic world, and all the other boring, repetitive crap that fills your life. See - it hurts, doesn't it, when I deliberately use offensive language? So no more of it, OK? Steve.

Steve: I don't want not to be friends with you, Steve. But it's difficult... The church, and Inga, are so opposed to what you're doing, and every time Inga reads one of your messages, she's all upset and shouts and screams at me for being your buddy! She's starting to blame me for what you do. Stu.

Stu: Two things: Firstly, training Inga sounds to me a bit like training a slave: get your dick in there, and show her who's boss. And secondly, if she's reading your mail, get another user-id! Steve.

Steve: OK, you win! And what makes you think I haven't got my dick in her already? I think you're lonely, with only those slaves and blue-collar types who are the other draymen for company. So you'd better carry on writing to me, to let it all out. Stu.

PART 5

Stu: It was really good to see you again - but I guess I'll have to get used to sharing my old buddy now, with Inga. It's a pity you could only make it for the weekend, and even then your mom and dad used up so much time. I was hoping to take you to see my slaves, as I'm really proud of them and the way they're shaping up. It's a pity Inga was so very rude when we were sitting on the porch, just like old times, and I started to tell you about them - I don't want her to come between you and me, Stu - our friendship goes back too far. But it is going to be hard, if, after you're married, whenever we meet I can't talk about my work. I mean, the job a man does sort of defines him, doesn't it? I know she agrees with your parents and wants you to be a pastor, like your father, or some sort of "do-gooder" in the anti-slavery league. And I suppose that's only like my dad wanting me to be a successful businessman, like him, really. But what do you want., Stu? Surely now that you're away studying you'll have had your eyes opened a bit - being a dirt-poor pastor down here isn't the way you were meant to spend your life, I'm sure: you're cleverer than that.... almost as intelligent as I am!

Anyway, as the Scandinavian wouldn't really let me talk to you as a buddy, let me just catch up and tell you where I'm at. After that fuck of two, the ex-sergeant, the next morning when I had all the slaves neatly lined up, kneeling there with their backs straight and their butts resting on their heels, hands clasped behind them ready for feeding, I went along the line with the feeder and gave them all their morning ration of chow. I couldn't resist the temptation to further humiliate two by pretending to wrinkle my nose from the faint smell of shit coming from his hair - just to remind him, if a reminder was needed, that last night I'd fucked him - no, I'd done better than that, I'd taken his cherry, as I'm sure he'd never allowed another guy that pleasure - and then wiped my dick clean on his head. Then I turned and addressed them all, reminding them of the new rules - that they were not to have any, and I meant any, sexual contact of any kind without my express prior authorisation. I then went to say "But as we saw last night, you're not to be trusted - two and four were only punished as examples to the rest of you: I know most of you jerked yourselves off, and I want to warn you that if there's any repetition, next time it won't just be the cane, but a visit to the whipmaster. And as you're all so untrustworthy, and can't be relied on not to play with yourselves at night, I'm going to try to make it a bit easier for you: from now on, you are all absolutely forbidden to touch your own dicks and balls and asses at any time, any time at all. If you are seen touching those parts of yourself, you will be flogged. So whenever your hands move towards your dicks, you'd all better stop and think!"

I told them they could then all stand, and they did, facing me at "attention" (I'd found it relatively easy to use the military stances), so I gave the order for them to turn to the right, and march off to the showers. It seemed to help them to march like this, although there couldn't be a lot of "stamping" as their feet were now bare as I'd decided that having them wear work boots, as some draymen allowed their teams to do, was more trouble for me than it was worth. It was surprising how quickly the soles of their feet had toughened up and they now had a layer of thick, horny skin over them. Jon had advised me about this, saying that although it made the slaves look a lot more sexy to be working naked except for boots, it also tended to make them less careful with our clients' packages we were supposed to be delivering, as they could be less careful and toss them around knowing that if a package dropped, it would be unlikely to break their toes! As you know, I'm determined to have the absolutely best team in the depot, so I had to forgo the erotic pleasures of seeing these big guys just in their boots as there's no way I was going to allow them to be "sloppy" in their work!

I like watching the slaves shower in the morning anyway - there are always two or three sets of them in there, and it's a good opportunity to look over the "competition", as well as being able to have a chat to the other draymen as we wait whilst the slaves clean themselves - they have their morning piss and shit on the way in, as there's an area about three feet wide covered with bars, and the slaves crouch there and crap and piss before moving on in to the shower area itself. My guys kind of clustered together as they usually do and began to wash, and I watched carefully so that the moment one of them went to start soaping his pubes, I could rap out "Stop! You fucking slaves - it's only about two minutes ago I absolutely forbad you to touch your own dicks! Did you all empty your brains away down the grating as you dropped your turds?" They looked puzzled, and tried to get on as usual without touching their dicks, and when they looked as if they were finished and were starting to move out of the spray, I snapped at them "You fucking slaves - you're still dirty! No team of mine is going to go around with dirty asses and dicks - clean yourselves!" I saw their look of puzzlement grow, and so I went on "You're not allowed to touch your own dicks and asses, but that doesn't mean you can't help out one of your buddies - I want to see you all soaping a dick, and an ass, and I want to see it NOW!"

I did feel a bit sorry for them - I mean, they never showed the slightest trace of embarrassment at showering together, as I guess that's what they were used to in their barracks all their lives as soldiers, but they went to almost fanatical lengths to avoid touching each others bodies as they did so. Perhaps it's something the marines teach them, perhaps they're all afraid that if two big husky marines touch each others flesh in the showers, they'll realise that they prefer the manly feel of another marine to a woman; who knows!. Anyway, I had noticed they all never touched in the showers, and now they had to stand there and not only touch each other as you sometimes see football players and so on do after a match, with arms around their shoulders, but that they were going to have to soap each others dicks, massage another guy's balls, and even slide their soapy fingers down their buddies' ass cracks to clean them out after the morning crap! They started slowly at first, all very hesitant and tentative, and then they began joking about it as their soapy fingers slid along their buddies' dicks and probed down those magnificent muscled butts, and after a very few minutes it was as if they'd always been together like that in the showers.

They came towards me again then, smiling and grinning, but I told them to halt. I called two to the front, and said curtly "Are you properly clean?" and he said yes, and I rapped out "Liar! How dare you think you can try to deceive me - I've been watching you, and seven, who soaped your dick, never 'skinned you back and did a proper job!" I ordered seven over and told him to kneel in front of two, then, as we all watched, I told two to clasp his hands behind his neck to keep them well out of the way, and then seven to take his buddy's dick, and this time to wash it properly, making sure there was no unpleasantness lurking under the 'skin. I could see two gritting his teeth in a mixture of frustration and shame as seven shyly held two's dick in the palm of one hand, and then gently moved his 'skin back so that we could all see the darker-coloured, moist head lying there. Two almost wriggled and squirmed as seven teased and fiddled with his 'skin and head, and I knew he would be so embarrassed as he was exposed to view like this - someone once told me that it's the ultimate nakedness for a guy with a 'skin, to have to expose his head to view, in a way that us cut guys just can't appreciate. It was good - another step on two's road to complete slavedom, as he realised that even this last shred of his personal privacy was no longer under his control, but mine.

That night, Jon and I fucked another two of them, and the good thing about that - apart from the fun it gave us, of course - was that the four who we hadn't yet covered came to realise that it was only a matter of time and that their turn was going to come. I also observed two standing there clutching the bars, his whole body language screaming out rage and anger at what we were doing to what he clearly regarded as "his" men. Still, it was good to see that whether because of the threat of punishment, or because he was coming to realise that as a slave he had no effective control over what was going to happen, he remained silent. When we'd finished that and put the two slaves back into the cage, I stood there outside the bars and commanded them to kneel in a line, as if I was going to feed them. When they were all there, I told them that I'd decided to give them a small reward as they'd all worked extremely hard on the exercise machines that afternoon, and that therefore they'd be allowed to have sex. I saw them all instantly cheer up at the prospect of being allowed to jerk off, but then their looks changed to completely stunned shock and outrage as I said "So get to it - but, remember, you're not allowed to touch yourselves, so simply lean over and do the guy next to you."

It was two as usual - he was in the middle of the line, as if to act as the focus of all of them - and he said, quite politely, I suppose, but with a hint of irony in his voice "Thank you so much, sir. But we'd prefer not to have sex now." I looked at them, and said, quietly, "Does two speak for all of you?", and they all nodded and murmured assent. To emphasise how wrong they were, I slashed my cane vigorously across the bars in front of them. "You fuckers are slaves!", I rapped. "And the sooner you get to remember it, the better and easier it will be for all of you. If your owner tells you that you will have sex, you will have sex. You have no choice. You all agreed with two, and his wrong-headed thinking has earned you all a punishment. Stand up, grip the bars in front of you, and push your butts backwards."

They to their feet and stood there, knuckles clenched as they gripped the bars, and looking nervously at each other, wondering what was going to happen next. I summoned up all my courage and opened the cage and went in, scuffing my feet through the straw, and examining the bodies lined up in front of me. I went along the row, slapping at the butts of some of them who had not thrust them out far enough, and then said "Remember, it's disobeying me, preferring to listen to two, that has got you in this position!" I then went down the line again, this time slashing out at their butts with my punishment cane, laying one hard stroke across each half of each of the slaves' butts. The anguished cries of the first ones as I worked my way down the line made it far worse, probably, for the ones at the other end who had to stand there, gripping the bars, with their anticipation adding to the pain they knew they would suffer. But their training was working, and none of them let go of the bars, and when I'd finished I walked out of the cage and locked the gate behind me. "Right!", I called out, "Before I needed to punish you, I gave you an order. Now, get in line, and jerk off the guy next to you."

They were still reluctant, and I saw a lot of them instinctively look towards two, as if for guidance. But it was clear that he'd given in - or had decided that he didn't want to get any more punishment meted out to them - as he just shook his head slightly as if in resignation, and knelt down into the straw and then reached out for the dick of the guy on his left. It all took a surprisingly long time, actually, as some of the guys didn't immediately get an erection when one of their buddies began to stroke them, and following that, some guys do take a long time when they're jerking off anyway, don't they? But I did have eight nice slimes of cum sprayed out from the cage to lie there, wet and white, shining under the lights, on the concrete of the pathway. As they watched, I walked along, inspecting their productions, and I told them that for slaves, they'd produced a reasonable quantity but that I was not pleased with the time it had taken and that this was perhaps something we should practice. That produced another lot of anxious stares at two, who now had difficulty in meeting the eyes of the other slaves.

Apart from the times when I was directly "training" my slaves and the time spent discussing them with Jon, this was a pretty boring time for me: the exercise machines were almost automatic so for long stretches of the day I had nothing to do. We couldn't move on to having me take my dray out, as we were waiting for delivery of a new one from the makers in Tulsa, and there didn't seem to be any way we could speed up the process, in spite of my almost daily phone calls to them. Things only really got interesting in the evenings when I furthered my plan to sexually subjugate the slaves by fucking them, and after another couple of days Jon and I had done all eight between us. These men, all of whom had previously thought they were "straight" now knew what it was like to experience a dick, and it was interesting to compare their reactions. Two was bitterly resentful and angry, four was just a wimp, and the others all varied - interestingly, two of the men didn't seem to object at all as I mounted them on the horse, and when I offered them my dick to slather and lube, they sucked at it eagerly and with obvious relish. And instead of screaming and raging at the indignity of my taking their cherry, I found their asses almost welcomed me, and the only sounds were their sighs and moans of sexual excitement. I was so surprised by this behaviour that I went back to the office and took another look at their personnel files which we'd got from the Pentagon, and to my astonishment found they were both married with a couple of kids each. I asked Jon about this and he just smiled and told me it was pretty normal - the marines were full of men who actually liked sex with other men but who had to conform to the norms of the service and who therefore married and fathered kids, whilst taking every opportunity to really enjoy their buddies when on an overseas posting, or a training exercise, or similar.

I noticed that the two slaves who enjoyed proper sex, five and eight, always seemed to be sleeping next to each other so that they could experience each other, and that when told to "line up" they took trouble to get next to each other so that if I ordered the slaves to jerk off their neighbour, they'd be together. And it was to these two who facilitated my next step: almost as if under the control of two, or afraid of him, the other slaves never asked if they could be allowed to jerk off or anything, and their sexual release mostly came when I ordered one of the mass jerk-offs, or decreed a "free" night when they could do as they wished. But one day this all changed, and when I asked my customary question, eight suddenly asked if he and five could fool around together that night. I saw two give them a coldly furious look, as if he saw this as some sort of gross disloyalty to him, and later I went over to the security lodge and asked to see the tapes of the early evening in the cage, to see what happened once I'd locked them all in and left.

Two, five and eight were having a furious argument, with two accusing the others of letting down the service, and of being fags. Five and eight really tore into him, though, pointing out that he wasn't living in the real world - they were no longer Marines, just slaves, and different rules applied here. They told him that they had little enough fun in their lives as slaves, and that they were going to enjoy themselves when they could, with each other. Five put his arm around eight, and in full sight of two they kissed - only briefly, admittedly, but it seemed to me to be a pretty courageous thing to do. I thought two was going to lash out at them physically, and a couple of the others had to restrain him for a few moments, but then it all seemed to quieten down and five and eight found a space for themselves right against the back wall of the cage. I watched with interest as they kissed and fondled each other, then kissed more passionately as they stroked at each others dicks - they could almost have been Jon and me, as if anyone had been eavesdropping on our encounters in his room they'd have seen substantially the same behaviour. I couldn't help noticing that most of the other slaves were rigidly silent and still whilst all this was going on, as if they were listening and observing five and eight, and there was an almost palpable air of tension around the cage until the two lovers finally fired their loads and fell into an exhausted sleep, arms and legs companionably intertwined.

It was time then for two's next "lesson" and I was quite looking forward to having those big strong thighs spread in front of me with his pucker waiting my attention - I'd decided I was going to fuck him "buckaroo" again, even though that might be pretty violent because of the way two threw himself around against the restraints, as his obvious hate of what was happening to him really turned me on. I was however not confident that another fucking - or even a series of further fuckings - would finally "break" him, but what other choice did I have? I was mulling this over in my mind when I remembered eight and five, and my choices suddenly expanded.

That night I went down to the cage, alone this time, without Jon, and ordered two to come out as I thought it would add to his humiliation if he actually had to drag the heavy punishment horse over to where the others could see, rather than me doing it. He stood there then, looking so very unhappy as he evidently thought he knew what was going to happen next, and was therefore very surprised when, instead of ordering him to lie on the horse, I instead briskly told him to turn around, and then to raise his hands behind his neck. I used the restraint cuffs from my belt to hold his hands in position then, using the D ring on his collar to hold the cuffs in place. He began to look puzzled, the more so when I ordered eight out of the cage, locking it carefully behind him, and then put eight onto the horse and fastened the ankle and wrist restraints.

I kept two standing there as he and the other slaves watched me use some of the sun oil they were accustomed to, to thoroughly lube and stretch eight's ass. Then I slathered my palm once more with oil, and went and oiled two's dick - he was used to this by now, from the regular morning's activities before exercising, and so raised little objection until, suddenly, the realisation of what I had in mind must have struck him. As I stroked the oil into his dick he suddenly said "No, sir, you can't make me do this. I won't." I slapped his dick with my open palm, just catching his balls as I did so, and he winced with pain. "Won't is a word that slaves do not use, two. It's not even a word that ought to be in their vocabulary. You will do whatever I say, or take the consequences."

He pulled himself up to his full height and flexed his muscles and said quietly "Sir, I won't fuck another guy. And you can't make me. There's no way you can make one man fuck another." I just smiled, and stroked his dick again to make it go properly hard, and then neatly slipped his 'skin back so that his moist dick head popped out and I could oil that, too. "See, two - we're already almost there. Like all men, you can't help throwing a wood with the proper stimulation. And now all I need to do is take you over to eight, and present you to him, and then you can fuck away...."

I took firm hold of his dick and balls, and with that kind of "encouragement" I moved him, hugely reluctantly, over to where eight was still lying, ass open and waiting. But when we got real close, two began to resist, and in spite of my strong pressure on his balls he just wouldn't move - his features were all screwed up as he suffered that terrible pain you have when your balls are under attack, but it was clear that he was not going to move any further, in spite of my insistence. I realised I was in trouble now - I suppose I could have caned two's rump until it was red and bleeding, but even then he might still resist, as he had that dreadful totally stubborn look on his face; and if he did, I would have demonstrated to all the watching slaves that two had bested me, and it was his determination that had won out. That might mean that I would have to move to the next stage of punishment and order a public whipping for him, and that I didn't want to do, as the skin of the back, buttocks and thighs never really properly recovers and my team of dray slaves just wouldn't look good.

I'd begun to wish that I'd never started this, but I'm a pretty creative guy, and at once an alternative solution presented itself, knowing, as I did, that two regarded himself as something of a "sergeant" and felt responsible for the others. It was too bad for eight that he had got caught up in all of this, but then, that's life, I thought, as I took my punishment cane from its holster and began to methodically beat eight's butt. His screams were piteous - usually, as I've told you, I only give slaves like eight a couple of strokes as he's generally well behaved, but this time my cane rose and fell twenty times, across both his butt and his thighs, before I stopped and paused for breath. There was stunned silence in the room, except for the sobbing of eight, and I didn't have to raise my voice to make myself heard by all of them. "Right, two, this is all up to you now. I've punished eight for your failure to obey me: you slaves should understand that I treat you as a team, and if one member of the team fails to perform in any way whatsoever, the whole team, or any member of it, can be punished. Now, stop resisting me, and come over and fuck eight. If you fail to do this, he'll be beaten again. And I'll go on beating him until you obey me."

Two just stood there, shaking his head slowly, whether from disbelief in what I'd said, or in defiance, I'm not sure which. So I took the cane up again and gave eight six more stripes cross his already battered butt, then said "And now six more, to the thighs....". I was gratified to hear two call out "No! Please, don't, sir. ..." And I stayed my arm, holding the cane high in the air, ready to strike down immediately if I was displeased. "Please, sir, if you're going to punish me, punish me!", two went on, sounding very anguished. "It's not fair to punish eight for something that I've done....". I struck down hard on eight's thighs, once on each, causing him to scream again, and then in the silence broken only by his continuing sobbing, looked at two again and said "Two, you don't understand, do you? You're all just slaves, and there's no such thing as being 'fair' to a slave! You're all just my property, and I'll treat you all any way I want. But if you're really concerned about 'fairness', you ought to consider yourself - are you being 'fair' to eight by making him suffer this agony, when it's you who is failing to obey a simple order? You can make this stop, you know, simply by behaving as a slave should and obeying me. Now, before I start on eight again - and I think it might be interesting to tawse his calves this time, as an interesting variant on the pain he's already in - just get over here and fuck him! You know it's not a problem for him, as he likes taking dick. So obey."

To tell you the truth, Stu, I began to get worried as two continued to stand there, still shaking his head in that curious way, as if he was almost stunned by what he'd seen me do. I was only marginally afraid that two would attack me, as he was pretty helpless, with his hands cuffed behind his head. But I didn't want to have to carry on beating eight, as there's no point in permanently damaging a slave, is there? And yet, if two continued to disobey me, what choice would I now have after I'd started down this route? Any backing off by me and all the slaves would see that two was the stronger man and my authority would be ruined. I unclipped the tawse from my belt, and repositioned myself a little further forward by the side of eight, as you need a longer "throw" and different angle to use the tawse effectively rather than the cane. I raised my arm, and to my great joy, heard two call out "No, sir, please, don't..."

I stopped, and gestured to two to move forward. In spite of the incredible sexual charge in the air and the ring around his dick and balls, he'd gone soft, and I wondered if this was some new form of subtle defiance of my will. So I grabbed his dick and began to jerk him quite harshly, 'skinning him back and raking my nails across his sensitive head as I did so. He did, of course, go stiff, and leading him by his dick as if it was a convenient handle, I moved him right up to stand between eight's spread-eagled thighs, and then did that thing that I find incredibly sexy: I moved two's dick head up and down the smooth, sweaty crack between eight's butt cheeks, so two would feel that incredible sensation in his manhood. Eight's sobs were turning into small gasps of pleasure as I did this, and my own dick was tenting my shorts, I can tell you! Two seemed both reluctant and excited, but his dick was gratifyingly hard in my hands, so I finally stopped and positioned it right on top of eight's dark pucker. "OK, two - in you go!", I said cheerily, but the big male just stood there, and I worried that at this last hurdle my plan would even now fail. I wasn't going to have another "discussion" with him, so as he stood there, almost frozen with indecision, I quickly raised my cane and slashed at his butt.

Two hadn't seen it coming at all, and he surged forward with the shock of the cane's stroke, forcing his dick into eight almost all the way. Eight gave a satisfyingly loud cry of pain and pleasure as two's dick skewered him, and two's own cry of surprise, outrage and pain only added to my excitement. Two was now right up against eight, his thighs in close contact with the aching flesh of the guy on the horse, and I now went and stood right behind two, so that he could feel the cloth of my clothing pressing against his naked body. I gently rubbed the stinging marks on his butt, as I said into his ear, quietly, "Now, two, it's not so bad, is it? Don't you like the feel of that hot, moist ass gripping your dick? So are you going to be sensible now and do as you're told, or do I have to punish you and eight again - I know you don't care personally, but think about eight there: I don't think his ass and thighs can take much more of the cane!"

I could feel his whole body tense as he thought about it, and I pressed home my advantage, not waiting for his reply. "Come on, boy, just ease yourself back, and then go forward slowly again...", I whispered, at the same time gripping his firm muscled hips with my hands and gently pulling him backwards.

Of course once he'd got started like this, and had felt that exciting stimulation of his dick by an ass, I had no more problems. I stood there, "guiding" two in and out, at first somewhat reluctantly, but then, as the inevitable excitement of sexual stimulation took over, I was able to stand back and watch two begin to thrust more and more vigorously into eight. It was almost amusing, actually, to see this stud, who had protested so vigorously about engaging in proper, man on man, sex taking to it so readily! He was soon really slamming into eight, totally disregarding the effects on the poor guy's caned butt as his body slammed into the flesh with that characteristic slapping noise. Eight's own satisfied moaning as two had begun so gently now turned back into cries of real passion - you know how it is, when you're really hurting, but you're gripped by the overwhelming enjoyment that only a dominating, controlling dick can bring to some men.

In spite of two's apparent acceptance of what he had been made to do, I was glad that I had taken the precaution of cuffing his wrists to his collar, as once he'd finished and pulled out of eight he wasn't able to touch himself, and had to stand there with his dick slimed with his cum and eight's ass juices, as a couple of last drops of cum gently oozed their way out of his piss slit. I could see all the other slaves looking at him through the bars of the cage, and he could see them too, of course, and would know that they could see this indisputable evidence that he'd fucked another guy. I took pity on him, though, and knowing that it's uncomfortable to have your hands cuffed like that for a long period of time, I went behind him and slowly undid the cuffs, whilst whispering, so that the other slaves couldn't hear, "So, two, that wasn't so bad, was it? In fact, watching you, it looked as if you were quite enjoying it! If you were to ask me, I'd say that you realised that you actually like the feeling of an ass gripping your dick..... But, anyway, it doesn't matter: what does matter is that you're a slave, and if I tell you to fuck one of the other slaves, in future you'll obey. The only consequence if you don't will be a whole lot more unnecessary pain and suffering for your companions - just think, if you hadn't defied me, you could have fucked eight without having made him go through all that unnecessary pain. Remember that, and act properly in future!''

I made two undo eight from the horse, and then I watched as two tried to apologise to the guy as they walked back into the cage - two had to help eight, as he could barely stand upright from the beating he'd received, and two was kind of slumped as he shepherded his companion along, as if he was ashamed of what he'd done. But was he ashamed of having fucked eight, or of having put eight through that beating? I just couldn't tell. Still, I went home that night really pleased that I'd made real progress at last - as I left, I told all the slaves that they were free to fuck or do anything else they wanted to that night, and I was looking forward to reviewing the video tapes the next morning to see what they got up to.

Look, Stu, you're not being a very good correspondent recently - I'm writing all this stuff to you and although my life must be pretty exciting at this point, surely there are things you're doing that are worth reporting to your old buddy..... Steve.

Steve: Sorry, mate, but I'm just so overwhelmed with all the work here at the moment. It's OK for you to sit down and type a few pages to me, but I have to spend hours at the PC anyway, researching and writing my class papers, and when I've got time to relax all I want to do is go over to the gym and throw myself into some hard physical exercise. And anyway, compared to your life, mine is pretty dull - classes all the time, then study groups, writing the fucking papers: it's a real slog., And no slaves to do it for me. And such spare time as I do have I'm spending with Inga, of course - sorry, buddy, but the thrills of writing to you just don't compare with being with Inga. But don't worry - I'm not going to give up on you: I love Inga, and I think we're going to get hitched, but that's no reason why we can't carry on hanging out together and "talking" like this. Do tell me what else is going on. Stu.

Stu: Well, the next big excitement is that my dray has arrived! When I got to the depot the next morning   never got chance to review the tapes of the cage from that night as I was told that overnight it had come by the long-distance carrier. It's a kit they send you, really - the big, long flat bed, the sides that need to be screwed on, the axles have to be fitted into their brackets underneath, the wheels bolted on to the axles, and then the driver's seat fitted, to top it all off: I don't know if you've really looked at a working dray, Stu, but there's a nice driving seat at the front, high up above the slaves, so you can get good access to the backs and butts of both rows of slaves when you need to "encourage" them with the driving whip. And before you start writing to me again about how "cruel" it is to whip the slaves, relax - it's not a whip in the sense of the bull whips they use when a slave is really being punished. No, it's more of an "inducement" to them to keep working away - a very long, thin flexible cane with just a couple of feet of leather strap at the end: it stings, really stings, when it makes contact, but does no permanent damage at all. Most draymen don't really use it much at all, as it's more of a "show" thing to reassure pedestrians and customers that you're properly in control of the slaves. But of course it can come in useful when you've got a full dray and you get to that big hill on Piney Ridge Road - they tell me that even the strongest teams begin to falter as they get about three quarters of the way up, and you just need to "encourage" them then so that their bodies give up the residual energy the brain keeps locked away against emergencies. It's another of those things in the management of slaves here: as Jon says, "you need to be cruel to be kind". What he means, I guess, is that without the carriage whip the slaves would falter and stumble, and then the dray might even start to slide backwards, and they might get hurt. It's kinder to them to "encourage" them to get to the top, to avoid all of that.

When I got to the cage, though, and had the slaves come out and kneel to be fed, it was obvious there'd been some vigorous "discussion" the previous night, after I'd left: two was sporting a huge black eye, and his butt and back were bright red and there were various other bruises all over him. It seemed to me that the others had perhaps "paid him back" for having put eight through all that totally unnecessary suffering. I resolved to go and look at the tapes as soon as I could, as I would be intrigued to see whether they had just beaten him, or had gone the whole way and fucked him, too - I wasn't going to ask, of course, as a drayman normally doesn't show concern for the physical well-being of his slaves, except or at the morning physical inspection. I got a particular pleasure from really squeezing two's body as I did this daily ritual, feeling him wince and shuffle as my fingers probed at the red patches and bruises that covered him, and gasp as he tried to suppress any sign that he was in pain. Then, when I ran my finger around his collar, as I always do, and asked him about the black eye, he just mumbled "I stumbled in the cage, sir, and fell awkwardly against the bars." I smiled inwardly to myself at this pathetic attempt to conceal from me that he'd taken a beating from his colleagues, and was pleased that the other slaves had shown him their displeasure - two was such a big guy that I doubted that he could have been than damaged if almost all the others had to ganged up on him.

I thought they all deserved a reward, so I told them to kneel again in a line, and went down putting a tiny "slave treat" into each mouth as they lolled their tongues out eager to receive it. I don't suppose you've ever been into a shop that specialises in slave accessories - uniforms, punishment devices, that sort of stuff - but amongst the other things they sell are these "treats" which you can use to reward your slave when he's done particularly well and gone beyond what you'd hope a slave would naturally do. They about the size of a cent coin, but very thin, and are just some sort of hard wafer impregnated with the most intense fruit flavour. You drop one of them on the slave's tongue and he at once gets his mouth filled with a taste that he's forgotten (assuming you feed the salves on concentrated chow, as we do), and they start to salivate and lick their lips and so on. They really enjoy it, and it does them no harm as it's just the flavour, so sugar or anything. Of course you need to use them sparingly, as although they are inexpensive (about fifty for a dollar) they really should only be used exceptionally - I mean, a slave's standard of performance ought to be exemplary, oughtn't it? You don't want the slave to get into his mind that every job completed deserves a reward - just on those occasions when, like now, they'd done something exceptional.

Finally, I told them that they could prepare the dray for action, instead of having another day on the exercise machines, and they almost cheered at this welcome break in the r routine.

I'll write again later, Stu, as I want to go and visit Jon. Steve.

PART 6

Stu: Hey, I've had a great day! Rather than wait whilst the mechanics at the depot got their lazy asses together and found time to assemble my dray, I decided to let my slaves do it. Funny that - I've started to think of them as "my" slaves, even though they belong to the company. Maybe this bonding thing is getting to me, and it's some sort of two-way process. Anyway, rather than have them waste another day on the exercise machines, I told them they could put the dray together themselves, and before long all eight of them were swarming over the packing crate it arrived in, then beginning to assemble it. It was kind of erotic, actually, to see eight totally nude guys working away - I mean, I'd been used to seeing them exercise and so on, but that's really different from seeing guys WORKING in the buff! For one thing, there's always an interesting interplay of muscles as they move their bodies in all sorts of ways, and for another, there are some parts of every task where two or more of them need to work closely together and so their bodies are touching. Add in a generous helping of sweat, as some parts of the dray, like the flat-bed and the axles, are really heavy, and you have the perfect recipe for making my shorts tent out very visibly.

It took the most of the morning - you know how it is with any kind of "flat pack" stuff: there's a set of instructions that appear to have been translated from Japanese by someone without a command of either Japanese or English! So there were lots of false starts, with bits being attached in the wrong way and so on. But, as I watched, it became clear that order was being created and things were progressing - two had the instructions in his hands and was rapping out orders to the others, who were obeying him. I guess it was his background as a sergeant that naturally made him assume control of "his" squad, and I have to say it really did work to get the task completed. Mind you, I wasn't all that happy about seeing two begin to reassert himself, after I'd taken so much trouble to "tame" him and make him a slave just like the others.

When it was done I was especially pleased to see the slaves taking a real pride in their work - they didn't just assemble the dray, but went over to the workshops and borrowed buckets, cleaning rags and polish, and gave the whole thing a thorough going over so that it absolutely sparkled and shone in the sunlight - it must be the military's love of "spit and polish" coming through, I think. I was so pleased that I told them to kneel, and went along the line giving them one of my "slave treats" as a reward.

I was feeling a bit sweaty and anxious, actually, as the time had come and I couldn't delay taking them out for their first run pulling the dray. I'd known that this was always going to happen of course, but I'd sort of pushed thinking about it to the back of my mind - there's a lot of worry, if you are really concerned: Will the slaves perform properly? Will they try to escape? Will they be rude to the customers and passers by? Will they obey my orders properly? Will I be able to exert the proper control over them in the streets as I've done in the depot? It's a big responsibility, you know - these eight big, tough, strong slaves, and the reputation of the Company riding on them as we get a lot of our business from repeat customers, and we don't want to upset them in any way whatsoever.

Whilst the slaves knelt there I went along the line and muzzled them - it's a bit of a matter of choice, as some draymen always muzzle their slaves, and some don't. I thought I would, at least initially, as it takes away one of the potential sources of difficulty in that whatever else happened it would prevent the slaves from being rude to people in the streets. It was a real shock for them, though: the muzzles we use are specially designed to allow them to breathe freely as they're working hard, so there's a circular plate with a hole in it that fits over the front top and bottom teeth and prevents the slave from totally closing his mouth, and at right angles to that there's a flat plate that stretches into his mouth and keeps his tongue pressed down. The combination of not being able to fully close the mouth and the depressed tongue means that any attempts at speech just come out as mumbled garbage! There's a trick to getting the thing fitted, though, as you have to get the slave to fully open his mouth to get the circular part over the teeth, and once you've got this done you take the side bars - flexible metal, rather like the arms on spectacles - around his head and snap them shut at the back, locking them closed. Once you've done that the slave can't get the plate off his teeth or tongue, and it's all done. I have to say that I fumbled the first few I did and it took much longer than it should have done, but when I got to two I was pretty proficient, and I really didn't deserve the cruel looks he gave me as I took away his power of speech.

I lined them up and took then back to the shitter next, as I didn't want any unfortunate incidents on our first trip out, and, to tell you the truth, Stu, I'd forgotten to ask Jon what we did about slaves who needed to crap or piss whilst we were out working. None of them crapped, as they were all now used to the concept of regular feeding and regular crapping, but most of them pissed, so it was worth the effort. I led them back out to the dray and for this first time I had them lined up numerically - one and two on the front left pushing bars, with three and four on the front right; and five and six behind one and two, and seven and eight behind three and four. They all stood there, their hands gripping the pushing bars in front of them, and I could see them wrapping their fingers around the smooth polished wood, as if they knew that this was going to be where they would be for many hours from now. We were almost ready for "the off", but I had one more thing to do: as they stood there, I went around taking a tether chain from its attachment on the dray through the "D" rings on each slave's collar in turn, closing the loop by attaching the other end back to the tethering point. There was now no possibility of the slaves escaping or even moving more than a couple of feet away from the dray. Equally importantly, they would see themselves as part of the "system": the dray and slaves joined together practically by the chain, but symbolically binding them into their servitude as part of the whole; they were no more important than the dray itself. Of course you can't work like this in practice, so the tether chain is really only useful in training: Jon says that some draymen never get to trust their slaves and therefore have to deliver the packages themselves, some allow one or two slaves not to be tethered so they can do deliveries, rotating the "free" slaves daily, but all of this makes more work for the drayman. Good draymen have their slaves properly trained so that the tether chain is only used as a mark of shame after some unfortunate incident, and all eight slaves can participate in heavy or bulky deliveries if necessary. Naturally I want to be the best, so my slaves will eventually stand there freely by the pulling bars, but for now, they would be tethered.

I climbed up into the driving seat and cracked my whip a few times experimentally - not to strike them, you'll be glad to hear, Stu, but to let them get used to the whistling sound it makes in the air and the "crack" the leather end can make if you jerk your wrist back properly. Then I gave them the order to move forwards, and with a fair degree of accuracy, we headed for the depot gates. I can tell you, Stu, I was really excited to be taking my dray and these magnificent slaves out for the first time - it was just like when dad bought me my first car, and when he then gave me the trap and slave I now prefer to use, only more so! But as we got to the gates and they opened and the slaves saw the busy highway thronged with cars, trucks, and cycles, with the pedestrians all over the sidewalks, they faltered: I think it suddenly occurred to them that they were going to be very publicly visible, very much "on display". They'd got used to being naked around the depot, in the cage and on the training machines, but now the realisation was striking them that their naked bodies, clothed only in their collars and cock rings, were utterly and totally exposed to all these people; and there was nothing they could do about it, as they were tethered to the dray, and they had to keep their hands on the pushing bars and certainly could not even attempt to cover their genitals! It ought to be a valuable lesson for them on their road to total slavery, as they came to realise that all a slave needs is his collar - a slave has no reason to be modest, no need to be ashamed of his body. If his owner decides that he should appear naked, it should be no concern of the slave as he is merely obeying his owner's instructions.

Anyway, they had their concerns and fears, and I had mine. I told them to pull out into the traffic, and turn left as we were going to head downtown. They looked at each other, knowing they were going to achieve maximum public exposure that way, but there was nothing to be done, was there? Especially when I cracked my carriage whip a couple of times in the air above their heads, to remind them I was firmly in control. I may have looked it, in my uniform, sitting up there on the high seat, but inside I was almost as scared as they were, but in different ways. A dray with its team of slaves on the pole out front is long and big, and it's fairly slow to react - the slaves just can't accelerate out of a potential problem, as you can in a car. Could I control these men, avoid danger to them and to other users of the highway? I decided to set a stiff pace right from the outset, and ordered a light jog, and by the time we'd gone through the seven sets of lights into the downtown area, they were sweating almost as much as I was! Fortunately for them, perhaps, the lunchtime rush was over so there weren't that many pedestrians to look at them as we bowled along, neatly in step (all that military training coming out again), and by the time we were out on to River Road I felt much more confident and in control.

As you know, Stu, I've had my own trap for a year, and I'd got used to the slave being able to take me more or less wherever I wanted to go in the neighbourhood with only minimal commands. I once tried to drive a real trap, with a real horse, on a "dude ranch" on vacation, and it was so difficult and frustrating: you have to guide the fucking thing every inch of the way with the reins, and you can't enjoy the scenery or anything. A slave pulling the trap is so much better (and your view of the slave's ass is so much nicer than the great rump of a horse!), and I suppose I'd though that driving the dray would be very much like that - I'd tell the slaves where to go, and that would be it. But of course it's all different in the heart of the city, as in going from the depot to "point A", there are different possibilities, and all the way along, given the mostly grid pattern of our streets, someone has to decide when to take a turn and when to continue straight on.... you can't rely on the slaves to do it, as there are eight of them and one might think that turning into fourteenth street is a good idea, whereas another might think it's a better idea to go on to fifteenth street before turning. So driving the dray is much more of a "hands on" experience than driving the trap, and I needed to keep my wits about me. There are compensations, though: instead of just one slave, you've now got eight beautiful bodies with big strong muscles working away in front of you!

I hadn't really meant to on this first trip, but once you're on River Road it's easy to find yourself suckered on to the off ramp for Piney Hills Road, and as we began the much steeper ascent I wished there had been an easy turn-off - but it's a divided highway, if you remember, for the first mile or so, and so I had no opportunity to turn around and we had to continue. The slaves were really starting to sweat now as it's one thing to jog along on the level, and quite another to jog up Piney hills Road, and I would have allowed them to slow down a bit except that I didn't want to delay the following traffic too much: my dray has the company name and an 0800 number on the back, and I didn't want a string of complaints going back to base from those drivers and their cell phones! So the slaves had to keep on jogging, and as they did begin to tire, they also started to slow down - I hadn't meant to, as I said, but there was little practical choice but to use my carriage whip for what it was intended, and I lashed out at the butts of the four corner slaves - one four, five and eight - to remind them that they needed to keep up the pace, and then, of course, I needed to do two three, six and seven as well, as they also needed "encouragement". And before you criticise me, Stu, let me remind you that this is a CARRIAGE whip, as I said, not a bullwhip. It stings - stings pretty badly, I should say, judging by the way the slaves jerk forward as it makes contact with their bare flesh - but it does no permanent damage. There's a red mark on the skin, of course, but that fades within a few hours, and other than that there's no harm done.

We've played there often enough, Stu, so you should remember that there's a turn off for Piney Hills Golf club about half way along Piney Hills Road, and so I allowed them to pull in there to get off the main highway. We went up the drive and into the parking lot, and I allowed the slaves to rest, and got down to take a look at them. It's a bit odd, really, to see them with these metal rings around their mouths and the "wings" holding them in place, but they were doing their jobs in that the slaves were breathing freely. We stood there for a few minutes and I noticed that the slaves were looking at the caddies in their enclosure at the edge of the parking lot - it occurred to me then that these ex-soldiers probably would never have played at an exclusive course like Pine Hills as they couldn't afford the fees (and when we went there, I always had to pay for you, if you remember, Stu), and so they would not have seen before the way that caddies are dressed at places like Piney Hills - or, rather, should I say "undressed"! Do you remember, Stu - they're totally naked, with only that small strip of hair on their heads and that stripe running down their heads, arms, bodies and legs? And the chain "waistcoats" that you can holster your clubs in, and which keep the caddies arms neatly at their sides? I said to my slaves "See, guys, you could have a worse job that being in the dray - how would you have liked it to have been inked like that when you were their age?" They couldn't reply, of course, but I think it's important to communicate with your slaves every now and then, just to show them you're interested in them.

It wasn't busy at Piney Hills that afternoon as rain was threatened, and the parking lot was mostly empty. It seemed to me therefore to be a good opportunity for the slaves to practice reversing the dray - it's not that easy, as the main pulling pole isn't rigidly attached to the dray but has a swivel fixing. So when the slaves move backwards, the dray tends to move in the opposite direction - it's like trying to reverse a car with a trailer on it! I knew that when we were "working for real" we'd often end up in confined spaces, and one-way streets and things like that, and so the slaves needed to have good control and be able to manoeuvre the dray in tight places. This was an ideal opportunity to practice, and I spend a couple of hours with them turning the dray in tight circles, and reversing it in to small spaces, which I marked out with piles of stones. I was glad to see how their confidence increased as we practised, and we were making real progress when the first drops of rain started to fall out of the sky.

It's not too bad for me - underneath the seat there's a waterproof for the driver, and a hat: it's like a big, long poncho that I simply pulled over my head and which was long enough so that when I was sitting down my whole body was covered, and the hat had a really broad brim all the way around to deflect the rain onto the shoulders of the poncho and not allow it to trickle down my neck. Rain is hard for the slaves, though, on their naked bodies: it's like trying to work in a running shower constantly, except that the water is cold, and with the big drops we get down here, they sting the skin when they hit. I could see the slaves already looking very uncomfortable as we set off, and before long, when it really began to pour down, I really did feel sorry for them as they looked so miserable. There was nothing to be done, though, as it looked as if the rain had set in for the day so there was no point in taking shelter, and, anyway, once we were working "for real" that would never be an option as all our deliveries are timed and you can't take a beak and wait for the rain to pass over. They might as well get used to our working conditions, and so I cracked the whip to indicate that they should move up from a jog to a run, as I thought it would be preferable to get the journey over as quickly as possible. We got caught up in the traffic downtown, though, as it always snarls up when it rains as you probably remember, and as we stood there in an almost stationary queue of traffic, I could see them starting to shiver as the cold rain cooled their skins down.

By the time we got back to the depot the rain was running off them - none of them was even vaguely erect in spite of their cock rings and the running, and the water was trickling off the end of their dicks just as if they were pissing. After we'd backed the dray into the storage building - I was proud of this, as even some experienced draymen find this bit difficult - I leapt down and went and undid the chain holding them to the dray, and pulled it trough their collars so they were free. They're supposed to stand there until given the order to "dismiss", of course, but I didn't have the heart to even think about disciplining them when they quickly huddled all together, running their hands all over each others bodies in a frantic effort to get some warmth back into themselves. So even though there was no need to, as they were clean enough from the rain, I marched them over to the showers and let them stand there under the hot water until they looked a lot better - at least with their gags still in they couldn't be accused of that thing that happens when you're frozen - there was no chattering of teeth!

Although it was still early there didn't seem much point in doing anything else that day in the rain, and I decided I'd quit early so that I could make it back home - I'd had a good day, and I wanted to tell dad about it - so I decided to feed them then and not wait until their regular feeding time. So I had them kneel in their feeding line, and as I was pleased with them I popped a "slave treat" into each of them before I inserted the feeder tube. That's one advantage of these gags with the hole in them - you can feed the slaves without needing to remove the gag.

When I'd finished, I ordered them into their cage, and they all stood there looking at me as I locked the gate, their mouths held open in that big "O" shaped rictus. Two pointed at his mouth and made a kind of desperate sound, and I went over to him. He gestured frantically at his gag, indicating that he wanted it out, and I gestured to him to turn around and used the special key from my belt to undo the straps holding it in. He almost tore the gag out of his mouth, and stood there looking at me. "Yes, two, you need to say something?" He looked astonished, and burst out "Sir, you can't be planning to keep us like this over night. It's bad enough being gagged and chained to the dray during the day... But keeping us gagged all the time, sir.... It's treating us like animals!". I looked at him and said quietly "Two, you just don't get it, do you? You are animals - slaves. You have no need to speak normally, and so why shouldn't you be gagged? It saves me the worry that you might have some unseemly outburst like this, and upset the customers. It doesn't interfere with me feeding and watering you as the feeder and water tubes go through the hole in the middle, and so where's the problem?"

He just slumped, as if my logic was irresistible, and said quietly now "Sir, please don't treat us like this. We are men, just like you, sir, and we like to talk to each other at night....". I stopped him abruptly right there. "You are NOT men, two. You are slaves. And I have decided that my slaves are going to be silent, and so for a few days at least I'm going to keep you gagged - I may decide that you're all calm enough at some point to be allowed to go ungagged, but that's my decision. However it does occur to me that you were good today in supervising the other slaves to assemble the dray, and it was useful to be able to speak. So although I'm going to keep the other slaves gagged, you may leave yours off so that you can continue in that role." I saw two considering this, and then, in what was clearly an obvious gesture of solidarity with the others, and of defiance for me, he put the gag back in his own mouth, and reached behind his head and snapped the fastening closed himself. He stood there, upright and proud, radiating his moral superiority, and I knew that I needed to do "something" to knock him back to his proper place.

I hadn't watered the slaves that night, so I fetched the waterer, ordered them all to kneel, and went down the line putting the tube in through their gags and allowing them all a nice long drink. When I got to two, however, I skipped over him and did the others. Then I went back to two, reached between the bars of the cage and slipped a leather thong around his neck, and hauled his head towards the bars so that his face was jammed right through them as far as it would go. I hauled the thong tight and knotted it securely, so two's head was wedged there. Slowly and casually, so that he and all the other slaves could see what I was doing, I got my dick out from my shorts and went over to the helpless two. As he saw what I was planning to do, two tried to escape, but of course his head was firmly secured and all he could do was kneel there. I pushed my dick forward and let it just go through the hole in the centre of his gag, and began to piss, very slowly. Two was making totally inarticulate noises as my piss started to fill his mouth, and clearly was not swallowing it as he was breathing through his nose and holding his throat shut, and my piss was trickling out of the corners of his mouth. Had it not been for the ring gas, I'm sure he would have bitten my dick off! His whole attitude annoyed me, so I took a firm hold of his nose and squeezed his nostrils closed so that he could only now breathe through his mouth, a mouth full of piss that he'd have to swallow to clear the air way.

I carried on pissing and could see two's Adam's apple working away desperately as he alternately gulped down air and swallowed my piss, and tears were welling up in his eyes, which I could see as I looked down at him as he knelt there in front of me, now once again humbled. When I'd finished and squeezed my dick to expel the last drops of my piss into his mouth, I wiped my dick head along his upper lip so that the last remaining traces of my piss were left right under his nostrils (as I did this of course it tingled with the excitement as two's growth of beard from that day scratched at t, and I had to exert all my self control to prevent myself getting an erection). I tucked my dick away, and undid the thong holding two, who now just continued to kneel there. I walked away from them all, without even a backward glance.

It was good to be home again that night - I'd spent a lot of time at the depot recently. As it was raining, I'd called up and had my pony bring the trap down to the depot so I didn't have to walk to the street car line; so I put on my big poncho and hat again and went out to where he was waiting - shivering, as my slaves had been earlier - even though he'd managed largely to get shelter from the rain under an overhanging doorway. We might have waited an hour or so for the rain to stop, but I was anxious to get home though, as it had been a tiring day. In my hurry, I practised my newly-acquired carriage whipping skills on him: previously I'd only used a tawse on his back if he ran too slowly, and he was kind of used to this, and it was gratifying to see the additional spurt of speed he was capable of mustering each time the end of my carriage whip snaked out and caught his butt - you probably remember, Stu, that my trap pony has deliciously long legs and a real "bubble" but, as dad chose him more on the basis of speed, rather than endurance like the dray slaves have.

It was much the same as ever that night, though - I was bubbling over and wanted to tell dad all about how I was getting on, and the huge progress I was making in "taming" my slaves and turning them into a proper working dray team, and dad just wasn't interested! He'd made me do this fucking job, after all, and now he just cut me short so he could sit there and tell me what a dreadful day he'd had in his endless meetings, and bore me with another of his incessant lectures on the prudent financial management of large corporate ventures. I always think that he never pays me enough attention, and he doesn't so much want a son, as an heir to carry on the business.... And it's not the same thing. Steve.

Steve: Parents can be difficult, can't they? Your dad has always been nice enough to me, but then I've only seen him occasionally when I've been a guest at your house and I suppose our innate southern hospitality and politeness has made him pay attention to me as a guest (even if I was only there as one of your buddies!). But he must love you, Steve, or at least have some plan for your future which might be his way of expressing his love for you: why else would he want you to do all this dray stuff? And don't you think he's working away for you, behind the scenes? I mean, does every new drayman, even if he's not as young as you, get a kind of "personal advisor" like this Jon? How much time is Jon taking form his other duties to act as a kind of mentor and advisor to you - it sounds like a lot, from what you write, and he must have your fathers' permission for that, surely?

I know that in the past you've often said to me that you wish you were me, with my dad as yours as he's so kind and considerate. You don't know the half of it, Steve - he's like that to you, on the outside, as he sees you as a "sinner" and he thinks that if he spends time with you, gets to know you, and empathises with your problems, he might get a chance to "save" you for Jesus. I know you well enough to know that it won't work, of course, but my dad will keep trying as he's happier when he's "saving" a lost soul than he ever is when he's dealing with his own son. He never spends any time with me, just as your dad doesn't with you, as he's always too busy sorting out problems in the church, or problems for his flock, or, if he's finished with those, down on his knees praying. So don't think that I get it all good, and you get it all bad.

I still think your dad made a mistake, though. I can't believe all this "training" of those dray slaves is really doing you any good - look at how you told me you whipped your pony to make him get you home quicker, and how you were unconcerned that he was wet and cold - I seem to remember that just after you'd got him you'd hardly touch him with the tawse, and when we were both in the trap one day with our golf clubs and we got to the bottom of Piney Hills Road, you made me get out and walk as two guys plus two sets of clubs would be too much for the poor creature! I guess these days you'd just lash at his butt two or three times, wouldn't you? It's making you hard and uncaring for your fellows, Steve. Watch it! I do care about you, and don't want all this to go horribly wrong for you. Stu.

Stu: You've got it all wrong! It's not making me "hard" at all - it's just making me realise that for the last couple of years my pony had it fucking easy! He's perfectly capable of taking two of us plus two sets of clubs up Piney Hills Road, and all he needs is "encouragement" to see that. It doesn't do a slave any good to know that his owner is soft on him - slaves appreciate owners who are fair, but firm, Stu - Jon says so. Anyway, let's not argue about this, as when you come in a couple of weeks time you'll see that I'm still the same old Steve you always knew, and I really am looking forward to showing you the dray this time.

Anyway, the next morning I was there bright and early to feed and water the slaves, and get them ready for our first real day of work. I ordered them to jerk off as I didn't want them always erect as we went about our business, and I especially didn't want any of them who hadn't had sex for a few days starting to drip pre-cum or even spontaneously ejaculate. It was good to see that they now did this as if it was absolutely normal to kneel there in a row and jerk off with your buddies, and afterwards I emphasised to them that they were to really empty themselves in the shitter, as I'd certainly punish any slave who needed to disrupt the day's work once we'd left the depot. Once they'd showered and shaved I did my morning inspection, even more carefully than usual, and I dished out some of the sun oil and told the slaves to massage it well into the skins of their buddies - I wanted my slaves to look really great, with their skins glowing with a healthy sheen, and this would do it - but only if it's well massaged in, of course, as otherwise you get a horrible shiny greasy mess. And then we marched out to the dray shed, and I was distressed to see that I didn't look all shiny and new any more - I'd been so stupidly concerned for the slaves being cold and wet the previous evening that I'd let them go straight over to their cage and hadn't taken the time to get them to clean it off properly - so we had to waste time now, valuable time at the start of the working day, whilst they completely cleaned and polished it again.

The consequence of this was that the others had started to arrive, and so we were now fourth in line to be loaded up by the warehouse slaves. It's a skilled business, actually - ideally, of course, you'd load the packages in the reverse order from that which they were to be delivered in: as the drayman, I get a palm-PC with all today's deliveries and routes in it, downloaded from the warehouse systems. All I need to do is follow the route, taking the last package off the dray each time and delivering it as we make a smooth, least-effort route around the city. But practical considerations of loading the dray come into play - you can't put very small packages marked "fragile" in front of big, heavy ones in case there should be a sudden halt that would cause everything to slide forward and crush the fragile stuff, and so on. So loading the dray takes longer than you'd expect, and it was irritating to be back in the queue and to have to wait.

Once loaded we headed for the gate - the slaves were now finding it a lot harder than it had been yesterday, and as we got there I decided it was probably unnecessary to keep them muzzled, and I anyway needed to do something about tethering them. I realised I could further my plan to break two and so achieve multiple objectives, and I told them to rest for a moment, and went around and took the muzzles off all except two - I let the slaves see I was putting the muzzles in the box under my seat so they'd know I could always muzzle them again if they were troublesome, and I turned to them and said "I expect silence - no chattering amongst yourselves, no making remarks to passers-by. You are allowed a polite 'thank you, ma'am' if a customer says you've done a good job delivering a package, but that's as far as it goes. If you break the rules, I'll muzzle you again. And you'll see that I'm keeping two muzzled as I gave him the opportunity last night to be free of it, but he chose to wear it! As he clearly likes wearing a muzzle, I'll let him continue."

I saw all of them look at two, and they were thinking that his defiance of me last night had clearly backfired on him. And it got worse, as I went on "I've also decided that I won't be using the tether chain for you - but, again, I expect you to behave properly. You are not to leave your assigned places between the shafts without my express permission - for example, when I need you to carry heavy packages. And if you do, you'll spend the rest of the week tethered. All except two, that is, who's rather unreliable: I don't want him spoiling things for the rest of you, and so I'm going to tether him anyway as he can't be trusted." So saying, I looped a shorter tether chain through two's collar, fastening then ends to the tether point, and then we were ready for the off.

They'd been embarrassed the day before at appearing naked on the streets, but they seemed to be less concerned about that today - perhaps they were getting used to the idea that my slaves were always going to work like that; or perhaps, and this is I suppose a little more likely, they were so focussed on the much harder job of pulling the loaded dray that they didn't have time to concern themselves about the prospect of someone seeing their dick bobbing up and down as they trotted along! They performed well, too - they were very responsive when I called out things like "next left" as I saw from the map on my palm-PC where we should go, and they maintained a good pace. We got to our first drop-off point, the goods inwards loading bay of a medium sized company, and I was proud of the skill they showed in backing the dray in so that I could supervise the slaves there to make sure they only took their company's packages off the dray. And then we were off to the next place, and so the morning passed relatively easily and without incident. When we had to make a delivery to a private home we tended to keep the dray on the street, and not back it into the driveway, and then I would take one or two of the slaves (depending on the weight of the package) to actually carry it for me, so I could focus on the customer and present the proper "face" of our company. I rotated this around, so that they all got a bit of variety away from the shafts, except for two, of course, who just had to stay there, tethered to the dray.

There are several well-known places in the city where our draymen and other delivery people from rival organisations tend to go at lunchtime (well-known to draymen, that is - I'd never heard of them before!) and as it got closer to one o'clock, I diverted from the planned route to go to one of them for my lunch. There were a couple of our drays already there, and I saw that it was the practice to allow the slaves to go and sit in the shade at the side of the parking lot, and so I told my slaves they could go over and join the others - all except two, of course, who just had to stand there, looking dejected and forlorn, muzzled and shackled to the dray. I don't eat a lot of lunch, but I chatted to the other draymen for a bit, and then went out to resume work. That fucking two had actually dared to sit down, and had perched himself on the central pole of the dray. He made no move to get back on his feet as I approached, and he needed to be taught a lesson he wouldn't forget - I hope you agree, Stu, and we're not going to have any more silly comments about "cruelty", but I couldn't allow this insolence, could I? Not only had he sat down, which is not allowed as he'd had clear instructions that morning to stay in place unless told otherwise, but he was completely disrespectful in not getting to his feet when his master approached! No slave master can allow a slave to get away with things like that, Stu, as it's not good for the slave - let him do little things like that, and soon you have a wild, unruly slave who doesn't obey properly and has to be sold, and probably sold at a lower price into some terrible new situation where his nature isn't so much of a problem, like down the mines. The considerate master corrects faults as soon as he detects them, therefore, and so without hesitation I took the carriage whip and started to beat two about the shoulders and back with it. I've told you it really stings when it hits the butt, but it's much, much worse on the shoulders and back as there's less muscle to cushion the shock. Had he been able to, two would have been howling with the pain, but as it was there was just this muffled kind of bellowing noise form him as my blows continued to fall.

I called the rest of the slaves back then and they looked pretty stunned by the whole thing, and I saw them looking at the vivid red marks all across two's back. Still, I had no more trouble for the rest of the day, and even when one delivery took an age as we had to unpack a new piece of equipment that was replacing a broken one so we could re-use the crate to return the broken piece to the manufacturer. When I got back to the kerbside the slaves were all still standing there in their assigned places, and had not dared to move! They were good guys, "learning by example", and I was even more pleased with having beaten two than I had been at the time: I now had a great deal of intellectual satisfaction with what I'd done, whereas at the time my pleasure had been purely in the physical joy of pounding the whip into male flesh. Steve.

Steve: No, I'm not going to go on at you about "cruelty". I guess you know more about "slave management" and what is, and what is not, considered "cruel", than I do. But I am a bit worried when you say, as you do at the end of your note "...my pleasure had been purely in the physical joy of pounding the whip into male flesh." Look at it, Steve!

That isn't the Steve I know - well, I don't think it is. I'll be worried about doing any of those things we used to enjoy together - wrestling, swimming, fooling around.... You may decide that you'd get "physical joy" from pounding something into me. What's happened to the Steve who was considerate and gentle? Stu

Stu: He grew up, and entered the real world. Steve.

PART 7

Stu: I'm glad we had that second phone call. When my phone rang immediately after you'd got that last message, we were both so keyed up that I though we'd never recover. So OK, it did take us almost two weeks to pick up the phone again, but then, we're both very strong-willed. And even now I'm not sure which of us backed down! I think we'd better agree to differ on this one - I'm certainly not going to change my view that my slaves are better off working on my dray than they would be down the mines, or still locked up in a prison camp. We agree, I know, that we couldn't just send them back to the north - so what are we going to do with all those rebel prisoners of war? It's not right to keep them locked up all their lives, and so making them slaves is the only other solution. There, I've said it again, and I hope that doesn't spark off another round of "discussion". And I promise not to make fun of the Jesus myth in future - I've known you long enough to see you grow out of believing in the tooth fairy, and Santa Claus, and so I'll hang on until the day that you finally see that Jesus is just another in that long line of inventions that amuse us in childhood but which we discard, with a smile, once we are mature and start thinking for ourselves.

Anyway, let's put all that bitterness behind us, and you said you wanted to know how I was getting in with my slaves, so here' a bit of a catch-up. Things went well all week - I kept two muzzled the whole time, and tethered to the dray whenever we went out - he was the only one like this, and I could see it eating away at him as he couldn't function properly in the way he wanted to, even though he was functioning perfectly as far as I was concerned: he wanted to be with "his men", and at lunch time and so on he couldn't do that as he remained tethered when they went off to sit down; and he couldn't give them orders, or even talk about their problems at night. But for me it was fine - he was a big, strong healthy animal pulling the dray, and his performance wasn't affected by the muzzle or tether - indeed, it was perhaps improved, as two's anger turned inwards, and made him work his balls of to "prove" to the others that he was still a "leader".

We had a problem on the Friday, though, as we were delivering one of those big double fridge/freezers with the ice-making mechanisms and stuff: they're really bulky, and fucking heavy, and this one had to go to the third floor of an apartment block and it wouldn't fit into the elevator. It only just fitted into the stairwell, too, and I told six of the slaves to get themselves behind it and get it carried up. These ex-soldiers work well under orders, but sometimes you need to be very precise and they don't always show much initiative, and I "took my eye off the ball" for a moment and they lost it! The thing slipped, and almost trapped seven underneath it - he'd have been seriously hurt if it hadn't just got wedged in angle of the staircase in the nick of time, and as it was, it still took ages to get him out, then to actually get the box up, and then to fill in all the paperwork as we'd damaged their building. As I stood there completing the forms for the block Super, I could see the other slaves telling two what had happened, and he seemed to be almost stamping his feet with frustration as he stood there, unable to speak. I realised that had he been with them, it would never have happened as two would have been "in charge" and would have made sure the whole thing went smoothly.

Perhaps I haven't mentioned it to you, but we work six days a week - well, only half a day on Saturday, as we mainly do "domestic" deliveries then where the householder has not been able to be home during the week. And on Sunday we don't work at all. It's not particularly for the benefit of the slaves, but as a benevolent employer we don't want to make the draymen work all the time, and we don't want the additional expense of hiring additional draymen to work some complicated shift pattern. On Sundays the slaves have to attend a church service, and there's a rota for about a quarter of the draymen to come in just to "supervise" the slaves as they stand there in the depot: we arrange for a pastor to come in and do it, so we can control the content of the service, and it's not particularly hard work for the drayman on duty as all he has to do is stand there with a carriage whip in case any of the slaves seem to be falling asleep, or fail to kneel, pray, stand, or whatever as the pastor tells them to do. See, Stu, religion does have some uses - we get the pastor to preach on the themes of obedience, rewards in heaven for those who lead a good life and obey here on earth, being kind and gentle and not violent to others, and all that other stuff that's in Christianity and that's really useful for keeping the oppressed in their places. Wasn't it Marx who said "religion is the opiate of the people"? - well, it certainly works for at least some of the slaves, as they seem quite fervent as they are ordered to their knees to pray, and perhaps it makes our job of controlling them easier. Mind you, the pastor had a bit of a job when he came to administer that sacrament stuff to two - he managed to stuff the wafer thing in through the hole in two's muzzle, but then two couldn't swallow it as his tongue was depressed, and the pastor seemed really upset when, as he tried to get the wine in (well it's not wine actually - we don't allow the slaves any alcohol, so we just use coloured water. But it makes no difference - if you can believe that wine transmutes to blood, you can presumably believe that coloured water does, too) he couldn't, and it trickled down two's chin and dripped down on to his chest.

After the service I locked some of the other sets of slaves in their cages and fed and watered them, leaving my own slaves standing in the yard. When I was finished I went back out and was pleased to see they were still standing in formation, two blocks of four, in their numbered sequence, properly at "slave rest" - they were managing to meld all that training they'd had in the forces with the ways of slavedom, and I was proud of them. I was going to take them back to their cage, but it was a nice day - the sun was shining and it was not too hot - and I had not much else to do, so I thought they deserved a bit of a treat. Jon would argue with me if he ever heard me using words like "deserved", as, he says, slaves "deserve" nothing: their only role in life is to obey and serve. But, as I said, it was a nice day and I was in a good mood, so I decided to take them out, down to the river park, for a bit of a change in their rather boring lives.

My first thought was to take the dray, but I had come down to the depot that morning in my trap and my pony was resting for the return home in the shade of one of the barns. I went over and told him to pull the trap over in front of the slaves, and then to wait for me on my return - he could have the afternoon "off" but I ordered him not to go into the barns where the dray slaves cages are as he's really keen on sex, and I didn't want him bending down in front of the cages so that he could take dick through the bars! I got up in to the trap, and said to the slaves "OK, guys, I'm going to take you to the park for the afternoon. I want you to line up in twos, and you'll jog in strict formation after me. One of you can pull my trap, and the rest follow. I pretended to scan the slaves, as if choosing which one to pull me, but I had of course already made up my mind. "Two, get between the shafts", I snapped, and as he came forward and stood there, I commanded him to kneel so that I could take out his muzzle. He knelt there, flexing his tongue and exercising his jaw, but not for long - although it isn't necessary as the pony is perfectly capable of obeying verbal orders, it's the fashion to always drive pony slaves with a bit, bridle and reins - you've seen me do it often enough, Stu, to know what I mean. So I told two to open his mouth, and then put the metal bit in, and fumbled and fiddled to attach the restraining straps behind his head and under his chin.

He probably felt this was much the same as the muzzle, but then I attached the reins to the end of the bit where they protruded from his mouth, and he began to look uncomfortable as he realised he was being transformed even further, from a big, tough slave down to something that was going to be steered by tugging on his bit! But worse was yet to come - I don't usually do it for my pony, but there's a ring under the strap that holds the bit in place, and I told two to bow his head, and then attached this to the D ring on his collar, so that he was unable to raise his head. From the box on the trap I then got out the blinkers - again, not something I put on my pony except on very formal occasions - and slipped the thin leather harness over his head and adjusted them so that he really could only see directly frontward. I commanded him to his feet and he stood there moving his head as if to try to see what was going on - his view was now severely restricted - and guided him to the small patch of ground directly in front of him, and told him to pick up the shafts of the trap. As he did so, I snapped the wrist restraints closed, so that he was held immovably between the shafts, and we were ready for the off.

I went and stood by him, and said, calmly, 'You're a trap pony now, two, and it's rather different from working the dray! For one thing, I don't give verbal orders - if I want you to turn left, I pull your head to the left with the reins, and similarly for the right. When I want you to slow down I'll pull back gently on both, and pull harder when I want you to halt. You speed up when you feel the carriage whip on your butt, and if I want you to run really fast, you'll know it as the power of the strokes will increase. Obviously you can't see much, so you have to rely on me to guide you - you have to trust me, two, and believe that I won't let you run into a wall, or under a truck, and I'll steer you around the bigger potholes in the highway. All you have to do is feel my commands through the reins and the whip, and react and obey: provided you do it promptly and well, there'll be no difficulty. But if you resist me, or fail to feel some of my lighter touches, you might be in big trouble - I only steer you around potholes with a very gentle tug, and if you go into one of them and stumble, you might break a leg. So this is all about trusting your driver, two, and complete and utter obedience to the smallest command.

I didn't give him any chance to reply or react - not that he could say much with the bit in his mouth, and went and got into the trap. I pulled the reins to position him towards the gate, and gave him a light flick on the butt with the whip to tell him to move off (the carriage whip is a lighter version of the dray one, and shorter, as it only has to reach the rump of one slave rather than four. These light "driving" touches don't hurt at all - they barely sting - but of course like any whip, if you increase the power of the stroke, you can really make the slave understand you mean business!). I could tell from the way that two was trying to move his head that he hated being forced to keep looking down, and straight ahead - he could have no sense of the landscape, or of turnings coming up, or anything, and he was absolutely reliant on my touch commands to perform. He kept shifting his hands on the shafts, too, although again the shackles holding him there prevented anything other than a tiny movement of an inch or so - it was as if he was now an integral part of my trap, just there to serve me, as were the wheels, or the seat. And he knew that any faltering, any hesitation, and the carriage whip would sting across his butt. I had finally reduced him to something that was even less than a dray slave - he was no more than a dumb beast, totally devoid of any means of independent action or thought.

At first I was concerned about taking my slaves out without even the dray to provide some degree of "control" - even though, apart from two, they were not tethered to it, it served as a constant reminder of their role and of the fact that they had the depot to go back to, and the resources of our company to hunt them down should they try to escape. Now they were just lined up in three rows of two and one at the rear, and there was nothing "binding" them to their normal role. They were just seven naked men who were expected to run behind my trap, and I was concerned that their sense of freedom might get the better of them and they might run off - it's pretty pointless, of course, as with those heavy slave collars on they aren't going to get very far: no one is going to use heavy machinery or an arc torch to take a slave's collar off, and they can't board a bus at the bus station, or a train at the train station without going through a metal detector that the collar will surely trigger, and they'll be caught. But nevertheless it's a risk - if they did do anything foolish, when they were recaptured we'd have to have them whipped, seriously whipped by the bull whip, and then they just wouldn't be the same - not only does their back never really recover, but somehow once he's been whipped like that a slave loses that little "something" - such small amount of independence he's allowed as a slave is totally dissipated and he's dull and totally lifeless and cowering - not something I wanted in my slaves. Still, I've seen on the TV how marines train sometimes, and I guess these columns of slaves were not all that different from the way that platoons of marines jog along - except, of course, that their bodies are covered.

I kept casting occasional glances behind me as we went along the highway towards the city centre, but the slaves were performing well, jogging along behind my trap, with their dicks neatly bobbing up and down. I suppose I could have had them run in front, so I could keep an eye on them, but then I couldn't have the pleasure of "steering" two by tugging on his reins and guiding him where I wanted to go - I'd have had to have shouted orders to the leading slave. Now, at least, I had two's sweating body in front of me, his powerful butt and thigh muscles pounding away, and the spread of his shoulders and the taut muscles in his back all accentuated by the fact that his head was bent, held there by the strap to his collar. It was a magnificent sight, and I flicked casually at his butt to speed him up, enjoying seeing how he was spurred forward as the sharp stinging tip of the whip caught his cheeks.

My trap is very light, and I don't suppose it was any harder for two to pull it than it was for him to take his one eighth share of the effort of pulling the loaded dray, but I sensed that for him this was the hardest work he'd ever done in his life - he couldn't toss his head proudly for relief, or spit a huge gob to clear his mouth. He couldn't vary his grip on the pulling bar, or reach down to scratch an itch, or even wipe sweat out of his eyes. No, he was totally helpless, there in front of me, unable even to see clearly where he was going and totally reliant on me to steer him clear of potholes and obstructions. He had to trust me completely and feel for the small movements I made with the reins to control him, and he knew that if he faltered, or slowed, the sting of the whip would be there to remind him of his duty to run at the pace I wanted. It amused me to make him go faster than he would have liked - a run, almost, rather than a gentle jog, as I knew this would tire him. It was bad enough for the following slaves, who were free, but for two the effort of the increased speed would be terrible, and as we stated up the gentle incline towards the city centre I felt I could sense the problems he was having in maintaining the power and speed I demanded. The breath must be whistling in and out of him through the hole in his muzzle, I thought, and now I could see his back and butt starting to shine in the hot sunlight as the sweat ran out from him as if it was a glossy coating on an iced cake. I wondered how much longer he'd be able to keep it up, and at a stop light I could see him visibly flagging as his body bent almost double as he tried to suck more air in: he needed to learn valuable lessons now though, so I pulled hard back on both reins and called out "Keep your body straight two - a show pony, pulling his master's trap, always maintains good posture so that the public can see what a fine animal his master has!".

It's unfortunate in a way that from the city centre it's all downhill to the River Park as I felt that two might even have "broken" if I'd driven him at that pace much longer, but going downhill is a little more risky in a trap because of the lack of effective braking, so I had to slow down somewhat (and of course the load was much reduced). So two had recovered somewhat by the time we were going along the path by the river, and it being a nice day, the grassy areas were full of people lying around or playing games, and from under the cool shade of the trees a little further back there was the appetising smell of families' lunchtime barbecues. We were quite a spectacle, I suppose - although pony traps are relatively common, as are delivery drays, it was unusual for a man as large a two to be harnessed in a trap as most ponies are younger, and thinner; and of course you do not usually see a line of well-drilled slaves following a trap, as I had. So people stopped what they were doing and to watch us, and mothers and fathers were probably telling their infant children to remember to behave, or else they'd end up like those slaves over there, and even like that pony, who must be very bad indeed if his owner needed to keep him restrained like that.

In response to the possible sensibilities at having so many slaves mixing with free people on a Sunday, I drove the trap for a mile or so along the river bank until we had left the normal Sunday family crowd behind, and there were just a few couples well back towards the bushes, probably enjoying some semi-secret outdoor tryst. I stopped two out in the sun, but conveniently near a shady tree that I could sit under, and looped his reins around a litter bin so that he was effectively tethered there. From under the seat I took my blanket and lay down in the warm afternoon air, and then dismissed the seven slaves and told them they could go off and play, or swim in the river, or whatever, but that they were not to stray by more than 100 metres from me as if I called and they failed to come, they would be punished. Several of them clustered around two as he stood there, but there was nothing they could do for him as he was immobile and muted by his harness and muzzle. They stayed there for a while, as if to show solidarity with him, but after a time they all drifted away to take part in an impromptu game of soccer, and a refreshing swim in the river.

I lay there in the cool shade, watching two as he was forced to stay there in the broiling sun, and after about an hour, by which time I judged he'd be very hot, and his legs would be aching as he couldn't sit or even move very much, I pulled on my sun hat and sauntered over to him. He must have heard me coming, but when I ran one hand over his butt and with the other gently tweaked his left tit, he shuffled nervously, as if surprised. "It doesn't have to be like this, two", I told him. "If you were a good, obedient slave, you too could be frolicking round in the meadows here, and taking a refreshing dip in the river. It's only your own stubborn pride, refusing to accept that you are now truly totally a slave, that must obey your master's every order, that makes me have to treat you like this. If you agree to behave as a slave should, all this would be over - I'll set you free from my trap and you can join your buddies... But I'd need your assurance that you would obey me completely, just a you used to obey your officers in the service. I cannot and will not tolerate you dumb insolence, and your attitude. Now, is that a deal?"

To the best of his ability, two shook his head. "Very well", I told him, "It's of no real concern to me as you can remain tethered and muzzled for ever, so far as I am concerned. The cane and tawse will ensure you put out the amount of effort I require, and the muzzle, tether, and perhaps those blinkers, worn permanently, will ensure you are not too independent. It's a pity for the others, of course, as without you they are at risk." This seemed to stop him dead, as he at once looked as if he was taking an interest, and I went on "These men are used to having a leader, two, you know that. They're only simple soldiers, and they need a sergeant to keep them in order, and to make sure orders are properly obeyed, so they avoid punishment. Without someone like you to guide them, two, they'll get slovenly, and will need punishment; and they might even do themselves serious harm - have they not told you how seven nearly had his back broken when that delivery went wrong on Friday? What do you think happens to a slave with a broken back, two? Do you want your men injured because your stubbornness and pride is making you so intransigent? Still, it's your choice - as I said, I'm happy to keep you working as you are, and perhaps that's for the best: no arguing, no concern for what you're doing, just neatly tethered and muzzled - I can live with that. And I suppose the others will get used to the more liberal use of the tawse and cane that their increasingly lax behaviour will bring them." I turned to walk away, and there was mumbling sounds of protest from two. I went back, and rested my hand on his butt again, enjoying the warm wetness of his crack as I allowed one of my fingers to stray into it a little, and with my other hand I traced patterns on the firm wetness of his belly.

"Yes, two? Were you agreeing with me, or starting some argument again?" I could tell by the way his body was slumped now that he was not in the mood for further argument, and so I said gently "here, two, let's take the bit out for a minute or two, so we can talk." I fumbled with the straps holding the bit in his mouth, and could almost feel the impatience building up in him. Then when he'd moistened his lips with his freed tongue, he said "Please, sir, let me look after my men...." - and I knew I had him! I just stood there, with him helplessly shackled as I let my hands experience the richness of his torso and the splendour of his belly, and then to wander down to savour the delights of his manhood, and told him that it was completely up to him. I would release him, but only provided I had his complete and utter obedience. I finished by saying "You see, two, I don't really think that you've accepted that you are a slave, that your only role is to obey me dutifully and completely. I shouldn't need to bargain with you to allow you to look after my slaves - a truly dutiful slave would want to help his owner get the best possible service out of the others. It's still symptomatic of your wrong thinking. I'm not sure that keeping you muzzled and shackled isn't actually in your best interests - it's not much fun being a slave when you are constantly chafing against it and are not content." Finally, he broke down. He stood there, his head bent, now in misery rather than because of the physical constraints I had placed on him, and said "Sir, please con't do that. I hate it, sir, being muzzled and shackled. I know I'm a slave, sir, but I am a man, too, a man who likes to use his body. And keeping me shackled and muzzled is not good, sir, for you, or for me. I can manage your other slaves, sir, and I want to do that.... Please let me, sir... Please."

I nodded, and said quietly "I think we both understand each other now, two. I will let you run free with the others, but if there's ever the slightest resistance from you again, I will have you muzzled and shackled again, but this time permanently. And as a shackled dray slave working in a team, you would really have no need of sight and so I would think of replacing blinkers with a little laser treatment to your eyes, to permanently dim your vision. And to save you even attempting argument, a shackled slave could be muted, permanently, by the simple cauterisation of the vocal chords. So think, two, and obey - or take the consequences. This is your only, and final warning." As I'd been saying this, I'd taken the blinkers off him, and then I used my key to unshackle him. He stood there, and as a man does, even if he's a slave, he stretched reflexively, and I was rewarded by the sight of his firm, flat belly stretching as his arms went above his head, and his dick was inevitably tugged upwards: there could be no doubt that here was the absolute perfection of the male form.

"OK, two, off you go and organise those slaves - it would be better if they were to exercise by playing volleyball or something like that, or by swimming. Don't go far away - when I whistle, I expect you all back here almost immediately. Understand?" He snapped "Sir, yes, sir", and I thought he was going to salute me - but he turned and raced over the grass towards the others. A few minutes later I wished I could go over and watch the volleyball - the sight of those hard, fit slaves leaping around entirely naked would have been spectacular, but I needed two to know that I trusted him to organise these things for me.

At the end of the afternoon - or, rather, when I was bored and wanted to get off home, I whistled and two at once rounded up the others and they jogged over towards me, neatly in formation. This slave management stuff was going to be so much easier with two to organise things, I thought. I looked at them, and said "Now, which of you is going to pull my trap back to the depot...?" And to my surprise, two at once stepped forward. "Sir, I pulled you here and I have the experience and expertise - please allow me to pull you back, sir." At first, I thought he might be being sarcastic and that he'd need to be whipped after all for this, but then I realised he was indeed sincere - to two, it was some sort of special mark of respect to have me select him for a task different from the others, and so as their leader it was "his right", irrespective of whether it was hard work for him.

After I'd fed them and locked them in their cage that night, I decided to have a little celebration, and went over to Jon's for the evening. He sensed my happy mood, and when he asked me why, I just said "Oh, things are kind of shaping up, you know. I'm getting the hang of these slaves, and so life is a lot easier than it was!" He looked at me for a minute, then slapped my butt, and said "So let's see if we can't make it just a little harder, then!". Steve.

Steve: That's not the way it works! You humiliated that two in front of his fellows, and at some point it will rebound on you. He's just obeying you because he's afraid of you - and who wouldn't be, when you've threatened to have him blinded! Take care, old buddy - you may be heading for big trouble here. And what did you mean when you said "Jon slapped me on the butt...."? Stu P.S. I've posted you the manuscript of my new epic "Consequences" - it doesn't look right in an e-mail as the indentation of the lines is important. Stu.

Stu: I never threatened to blind him. I specifically said I'd "permanently dim his vision" - some owners have it done to all their slaves as it quietens them down - it just makes most things more than a couple of feet away be totally out of focus, like not wearing glasses. You wouldn't want to blind a slave - think about it: his value would be halved!

Now, about "Consequences" - I'm not an expert, and I'm more of a prose person than a poet, but I think I can see what you mean. The spacing of the lines like that adds a certain power to the feeling of emptiness and loneliness in the last stanzas that wouldn't be there if all the lines were packed properly. But then I'm no judge - unless poetry rhymes, I don't think it's poetry! But I'm glad you shared it with me - even though it makes me glad I'm not doing that sort of thing at college: I'm a tad more practical, as you know. Still, I'll keep it safe - if you ever get to be another T S Eliot or Sylvia Plath, it will be worth real money!

I might even have time to write something myself - but a story, or even the first chapters of my autobiography (I may as well get it out of the way now, as it's happening, as I have this feeling that I'll be famous, ha, ha.) - with two now effectively ' running things" when we're out delivering, and constantly inspecting and monitoring the slaves in the depot, I've not got all that much to do. He chides and kind of "nudges" the others into the correct behaviour, and is an absolute stickler for them being neat and smart at all times - his background as a sergeant helps, and even though they are all technically the same, all slaves together, the others don't seem to resent him doing this in any way.

I suppose it's all their training as soldiers, when a sergeant was an authority figure, who they obey instinctively. Steve.

Steve: You? Write? Don't make me laugh! You've got no creative imagination and don't use imagery. Don't get me wrong, old buddy, I like you, and you're great to go out partying and drinking with, but you're just not "creative" - artistically creative, that is. I doubt that you could string a story together, let alone a poem. Stu

Stu: Of course I can write! Look back at our correspondence. I'm telling you a whole lot more about my life than you are telling me about yours. When we had to sit through all those endless dissections of famous poets and their work at high school I always thought they were arrogant.... You're at least qualified on that score to be one, then! But don't stop - when I do my memoirs, I can always say "And before he had that string of lovers that his poetic temperament suited him for, he had me. My hand was the first to make love to him...." There - isn't that poetry? What an image! Steve.

P.S. Have you actually fucked the Scandinavian yet? Steve.

Steve: Ha fucking ha! "Making love to your hand" is hardly a poetic image. Even though it makes the trouser snake stir a little at the thought. And don't ask such personal questions, not even to your best friend. What happens between Inga and me is our business. Stu.

Stu: So you haven't, then (fucked her, that is)! Steve.

Steve: Mind your own business. Stu.

Steve: Where are you, buddy? When I said "mind your own business" I didn't mean for you to go totally silent. Come on, I want to hear more about those slaves of yours. Stu.

Stu: I don't know how to write this. It's really hard. But if I don't tell someone, I'll go mad. Maybe putting it down on paper will make it better. I just couldn't even bear to sit at the screen these last three days. And just when everything was going so well.

Look, it was late. I'd fed and watered my slaves and caged them, then gone to have a little talk with Jon, and was about to go home when I crossed the yard and there was a team of slaves just standing there, in the dray. It was raining, and the poor guys were all huddled together, trying to keep warm (I've told you how ra n is the enemy, even on a relatively warm day). They were the team that that big guy I told you about - the one who hauled the bar tender across the bar - drove, and it was always whispered (although not in Matt's presence) that he didn't look after them very well, and was unnecessarily harsh with the cane and tawse. I knew where he'd be, of course, and by the time I'd marched across the road to the bar, I was pretty pissed off - these slaves are, after all, a valuable asset of the company, my dad's company.

I tied to be reasonable, and went over to him and said that I'd seen his slaves standing there shivering, and wasn't it time they were fed and caged. He put his beer down, looked at me, and just said "Mind your own fucking business!". I lost it, Stu - I was so cross that I shouted back "It is my fucking business! Those are the company's slaves getting cold out there, and they might come down with pneumonia, or something.... It is my business - it's my dad's resources you're risking as you stand here with that beer...."

That was it! He just grabbed me, slapped me a couple of times, and shouted "Mind your own fucking business! Daddy's boy, coming here and trying to tell a real man how to manage a few slaves. We've all seen you, treating those slaves of yours as if they were free men, almost. Keep your nose out from where it doesn't belong, boy." Well, I went for him, but it was no kind of fight - he'd huge, and although he's flabby, immensely strong, and taller and much heavier than me, and a few punches and I was a crumpled heap on the ground. As I lay there he slowly and deliberately finished his drink, as if he was in no hurry, then said to all the other draymen "I'd better go and deal with my slaves, I suppose. They need teaching a lesson - causing me trouble like this!". He turned and ambled out of the bar, and as soon as he'd gone, some of the others, who all seemed afraid of him, came and helped me to my feet. I stood there, hurting like hell from where his punches had landed, but I staggered to the door and across the road to see him standing in the courtyard just slashing wildly at his slaves with his punishment cane as they still huddled together in the pouring rain. I half ran over, as best I could, and tried to stay his hand, screaming at him that it wasn't their fault and to stop hitting them - he just lashed out at me then, and floored me again, then stood over me saying "I ought to cane you, you young puppy, interfering between a drayman and his slaves."

I though he was going to start caning me, and, as it turned out, that might have been the best thing to happen. I couldn't get to my feet, but I curled my arm around his legs and tried to pull him over. He seemed to lose all sense of proportion then, and reached down and grabbed me. He had me in some sort of wrestling hold that I couldn't break away from as he was so big and strong compared to me, and he half carried, half dragged me across the depot to the stairs leading to the BDQ where he and some of the other draymen lived, then hauled me up the stairs. I remember hearing his door crashing open, and then I was face down on his bed - it's funny, isn't it, but you mind takes snapshots of things that you can recall later, and I can remember seeing a hard patch on the sheet, probably his dried cum, and getting the sour smell of where his body had been lying on sheets that need laundering. His weight was heavy on me, and his head was next to mine as he muttered "Now you're going to get it, you little fucker - let me show you how a real man deals with interfering busybodies...."

He was so violent that he actually tore the buttons off my pants as he wrenched them down so that I was lying there half naked, and my shirt and T fared no better as he pulled them off me, not caring if he caught my ears or anything. I realised what he meant to do, and began to really struggle and fight again, but far from making things better, it made them worse - it seemed to inflame him, to drive him on, and he was shouting at me telling me that now I was going to get it.... And when I saw him dropping his pants and tried to get up and run out, even though I was stark naked, he just caught my arm, slapped me across the face with his other hand so hard that I almost passed out, then hit my ass twice as he threw me down on to the bed.

Stu, I don't know how I can tell you how awful it was. I'd always thought that to rape a guy you'd push him over something so he was bent at the waist, but Matt just threw himself on me. His one knee was pressing painfully into my right thigh, and that in itself was almost enough to keep me pinned to the bed, and his other knee was pushing my other thigh so far over that I thought I might split open. One huge hand was around my neck, and he forced my face so far down into the mattress that I thought I might suffocate. And then I felt his dick at my ass - his other hand was forcing my butt apart, and once he was satisfied he must just have pushed down with all his body weight, as there was no stopping it as his dick speared up into me. From somewhere I heard myself scream, or try to, as my face was deep down, as I've said. The pain was indescribable. And then, as he began to pound up and down, I shouted, raged, screamed and cried, all to no avail. I could hardly breathe as his huge body pressed down on me, and I wasn't sure I wanted to, as I hurt so much.

I'd always kind of imagined that a rape would be over quickly. I mean, in those stories, and in the movies, it's all over after a couple of quick pumps of the guy's dick into the woman, and if I'd ever thought about it at all, I'd imagined it would be like that when one guy takes another forcibly (not that you normally need to - most guys are happy to have sex, after all. But then, you wouldn't know that, Stu). But this went on and on - I was almost suffocating, and I was hurting: hurt like I've never known it before, as he remorselessly and ruthlessly continued to pump his huge dick in and out of my battered ass. And it wasn't like when I've fucked slaves - relatively gentle, and slow and sensual - no, it was fast, hard, pumping action and above the sound of my own attempts to scream I could hear that awful slap, slap, slap noise as his big body crashed into mine. He was grunting with satisfaction as he worked at me, and the rank smell of his stale sweat was nauseating. I hung in there with everything I'd got as I needed to remember this - I was going to have my revenge on him, and in spite of everything I was going through I didn't want to pass out as I needed to be able to recall it so that his punishment could match his crime.

Finally it was over as he gave a great shout and stopped pumping in to me. You know how they say in those stories that you could feel the hot cum spurting up into you, well it's not true - there are no sensors up there and you can't detect it, and the only way I knew he must have cum is because he stopped the terrible pounding of my body. But then he flopped forward onto me, and I could feel his big flabby belly on my back and his weight almost crushed the breath out of me. Fortunately he'd let go of my head so I could just about breathe, and he now put his mouth next to my ear and said "There you are, you little fucker! That's how a real man deals with a boy like you. Now you've had a real man's dick up you, perhaps you'll learn not to interfere in other men's business." The stench of his breath was foul, as he'd been drinking and the beer and alcohol fumes washed over me, and I felt like being sick.

He moved his heavy thighs and the weight of his body eased a little, and I took the opportunity to slide out from under him - we were both so slicked with sweat that it was relatively easy. But before I could make my escape he'd grabbed my arm and pulled me back onto the bed. "Come here you little fucker!", he roared, and before I knew where I was he'd sat on the side of the bed and put me over his knees. It was all a bit of a blur - being up-ended like that, and one moment I was standing, the next I was conscious that my eyes were staring at his feet with their horny misshapen long toenails. It was absurd, I know, but the thought went through me that a man ought to keep his toenails neat! But it was driven out as he began to spank me, his big hand falling repetitively on my ass. I tried to get away, but he opened his thighs and neatly trapped my dick and balls between them, and that, and his other hand around my waist, held me there as his huge, heavy hands beat me again and again. I'm not proud of it, but I screamed - no, squealed is probably more like it. I tried to stifle it, but the stinging violence of his brutal strokes really hurt.

Finally, he'd had enough, and he just pushed me off his lap and I lay there, sprawled at his feet. He was s laughing now, laughing at me, and this was almost the hardest part of it, Stu. "You think you're a big man, dealing with those slaves of yours just as if you're a proper drayman.

But you're just a boy, aren't you? A boy who gets put over a real man's knees and spanked if he's naughty!" I felt my eyes fill with tears from the pain I was suffering, but my anger was so fierce that I got to my feet and threw myself at him, my fists and legs flailing wildly as I tried to punch, kick or even scratch him. I saw his arm draw back and his fist coming towards me, and that was it.

He must have carried me back to my own room in the BDQ as I woke up lying naked on my own bed. There was cum and ass juice everywhere, and as I tried to move I realised just how much I was hurting. I managed to drag myself into the shower, but the face I saw when I went to shave was almost unrecognisable: I had black eyes, bruises on my cheeks, and all over my body were big hand prints and more bruising. I tentatively ran a piece of toilet tissue along my ass crack, and I almost screamed when it came away covered in blood. I'd never hurt so much in all my life. Steve.

PART 8

Steve: Thank god you were OK. I used up almost all the credit on my cell trying to contact you - the people at your depot didn't know where you were, and I called your home, who said you were at work.... And you don't carry your cell around: really, Steve, that's so stupid! What are you going to do if one of those fucking slaves of yours escapes?

I know you were pissed off at me when finally you did answer your cell and I said it sounded like poetic justice to me (no, that's not justice meted out by poets like me!). But think about it, Steve - what did you do to those slaves when you first got them? You told me you had that two, and the others, on a "horse" and then you raped him. And when he was disobedient you had him on there again and caned him - in fact, you're proud of your prowess with the punishment cane. And when we talked about whether that two minded having your dick forced into him, or was upset at being caned, you just said that he was a slave. So perhaps you now know what it's liked to be raped, and beaten up - think about it when you're dealing with that two and your other slaves. Stu.

Stu: For fuck's sake, it isn't the same at all. I'm a man, a free man, and that Matt raped me, and beat me up. What I do with the slaves is entirely different - fucking the slaves is part of the process of turning them from men into slaves - you need to do it, like you have them collared and tattooed and their pubes trimmed. And as for caning them - well, it's not like beating them up at all - surely you can see that? Slaves need discipline, and it's good for them - how else can they know that they've displeased you if you don't cane them? How else can they know that they're not working hard enough without the tawse or the whip "encouraging" them? I really am surprised at you, Stu, to compare what Matt did to me to the proper management of slaves. Steve.

Steve: Look, you and two are both men. And a dick forced up either of your asses causes you just as much pain, and makes you feel just as used, and takes away your sense of being a male. Can't you see that? Stu.

Stu: no, I don't see it at all. You only think that way because you don't work around slaves, and you don't have the responsibility for training and managing them. How on earth could I control big tough guys like two if I hadn't "broken" him, and if he wasn't aware that I could easily punish him if he fails to obey? Get real, Stu - physical discipline is the only thing that slaves understand, the only thing that motivates them. I can't give him a bigger salary rise if he works harder, or promote him, or anything like that, as he's a slave. So the only thing left is physical punishment. How else would you keep a slave motivated? Read him a poem?!

Anyway, we're starting another quarrel here. Let's just agree to differ on the problems of slave management, and let me tell you what I did to get back at that fucker Matt. I was still really sore - those bruises all over me; and I looked a fright, with my black eye and bruised face. And it was REALLY painful to have to sit on the dray, and to keep getting on and off to deliver the packages, as my ass was so tender and sore. And crapping was a real trial, even though it turned out that my ass wasn't torn (as it could have been, with that forcible entry) - the blood I'd seen that night was just the kind of stuff you get from "enthusiastic" sex anyway, even though it had been pretty scary at the time. Still, no one gets away with stuff like that when they're dealing with me.

As he did most nights, Matt skimped on looking after his slaves and went over to the bar. I chatted to the concierge at the desk in the hall of the BDQ, and asked him to go and get me another blanket, and whilst he was away I leaned over and took the spare key to Matt's room from the key safe. I went up and let myself in, and I almost panicked as I saw again that terrible scene - it brought my memories flooding back. The place was like a pigsty, with empty beer cans, unwashed plates, and dirty clothes strewn about the place, and there was the smell of unwashed bodies and stale food in the air. It almost made me gag and vomit. And I had to endure it for about two and a half hours, before I heard Matt getting back, and stumbling around in the hall as he was probably drunk.

The moment he came in I stabbed him with my slave prod, set to its maximum "stun" position, and he collapsed into a big sagging heap on the threshold. As I've told you, he's a really big, heavy guy and it took all my strength to drag him across the floor and onto the bed, and when he was there I hauled his arms above his head and cuffed his wrists to the headboard of the bed. As he's so strong and violent, I pulled his boots off, and the stench of his sweaty feet almost made me vomit yet again. I just waited then until he came around from the prod, and he was in some considerable pain, as you'd expect. But it turned to rage, the moment he realised that he was cuffed to the headboard, and that I was sitting there watching him. He shouted and screamed at me to let him free, and I just shook my head, and went and stood by the bed. He tried to lash out at me with his legs, and so I reached over and grabbed his dick through his shorts, and squeezed it and his balls hard: he really had something to scream about now, and I ordered him to be silent, and lie still.

"So, Matt, you like sex with other guys", I told him calmly. "So you're going to have a really good night tonight - there's going to be a lot of sex!" He started shouting again, being really abusive and using the type of language I imagine is common in the barracks room, so I shut him up by another squeeze to his balls. But when I started to pull his shorts off it started all over again, and I had to wave the slave prod in the air near his neck to remind him to be silent. Like all of us he didn't have underwear under his shorts, so his monstrous dick, the one that had raped me, was lying there like a fat, lifeless sausage over his big balls. I prodded at it with the slave prod (not turned on) as I wanted to show him that I had the power to seriously hurt him if I wanted to, and as I moved his dick and balls around with the tip, he gradually became erect. "So, do you want to fuck again, Matt? Do you want to force that big dick up me again?"

"Look, Steve, just let me go, will you, and we'll forget all about this....", he began, and I silenced him by tapping his balls with my prod, making him wince. "No, Matt - we can't forget about it. And, anyway, I wouldn't want to deprive you of an evening of sex!"

He watched as I tied a rope around his ankle and then looped it around the headboard of the bed, but when I started to tighten the rope to pull his leg up above his head, he resisted. "Now, Matt, be careful!", I chided him. "I think it would be best if you co-operated with me, don't you? Would you like the slave prod turned on?" He could see that he was helpless and in my power, and relaxed his muscles, so that I could then tie his leg in place, and I repeated the process on his right side so that he was then in the classic position for fucking - lying there on his back, legs spread and feet pulled right back. His hole was there, right in front of me, surrounded by his fat butt and the untidy mass of thick black curls that was his pubic hair. There was a nasty smell of shit and stale sweat, and, to tell you the truth, I really didn't fancy fucking it at all. But I'd thought of that, and the fact that I really wanted to hurt this fucker, so during the day I'd had the slaves stop for a few moments downtown whilst I went into a sex shop and bought a dildo - a monstrous, black leather one, one that cannot possibly have been modelled on any real life dick ever in existence! Look, Stu, you know that I've not got anything to be ashamed of as far as dick size is concerned, as you were always telling me how hard it was to wrap your fingers around it when we were fooling around together, and when we stood face to face and kissed, it was obvious that mine was so much longer even than yours. But I really wanted to teach Matt a lesson, and so I'd gone and bought this monstrous thing.

Matt's eyes almost popped out of his head when I produced it, and I said quietly "Do you want to lube it a bit, Matt? " as I moved it towards his lips. He turned his head away, muttering "Fucker!", and I just shrugged, positioned it at his hole, and pushed. I very quickly realised that his screams would alert someone and interrupt us, so I pulled his stinking socks off his feet and simply stuffed them into his mouth (squeezing his balls to make him open wide!). And then I worked on him with that thing - he tried to arch his body as if to get away from it as I slowly and inexorably pushed it right up inside him, and he was thrashing his head from side to side and making loud but totally inarticulate noises as I did so. It was really difficult, I can tell you - there's an incredible resistance to overcome if you try to push something that size up an ass without lubing and stretching! Then when it was right in, I didn't allow him any time to recover at all as I started to slide it in and out, all the time seeing Matt's body spasming, and listening to the terrible noises he was making.

The problem in using a dildo of course is that although it stretches the hole and can hurt terribly as it does so, there's no other physical sensation as there is when you fuck a guy properly - that additional hurt you can cause when you really slam your body hard against the sensitive parts of his, and I didn't want Matt to miss out on any of this! I'd thought about caning him, but had instead also bought a paddle, a long, very flexible one made of stiff black leather, and so I pushed the dildo up him once more and left it there, and then began to beat at those very sensitive parts of his body with this paddle. The "slap" noise it made as the leather made contact with the tender skin on the inside of Matt's thighs right near his hole was most gratifying, especially as I saw Matt jerk with shock each time it struck. In addition to the noise he was making, I could see tears coursing down his cheeks now, so I began once more to alternate quick, violent thrusts with the dildo with sessions with the paddle.

He was lucky that I bore easily, Stu, as I just couldn't be bothered to carry on for more than about fifteen minutes, but when I pulled the dildo out for the last time I almost restarted when I saw how much he'd been stretched by it - I just knew it must be almost agonisingly painful for him, and that he'd be completely humiliated by what had happened to him. I needed to do a few more things, though, so the electric clippers I'd borrowed from the slave sheds were used to quickly strip off the majority of the hair around his ass and pubes, and then I unbuttoned his shirt and ran them right up through the forest of his belly and chest, leaving a white trail through the black curls. I didn't really like having to jerk him off, so I pulled on a rubber glove to do it, and I simply didn't care that the friction this caused seemed to be making the shaft of his dick red and sore, even breaking the sensitive skin slightly so that there were red patches of blood on the glove! The white path down his body was then slicked with his cum, and then, as a finale, I went and stood right by his face and jerked myself off so that my cum sprayed all over his eyes, nose and chin.

It was like photographing the carcass of some hunted animal when I got out my digital camera and started to take shots of him - his ass with the dildo sticking out, his dick and balls shaved of their hair, the cum streaking his shaved chest, and finally the smears of my cum all over his face, and then I'd finished. I untied his legs, and then, as I went to untie his hands, I got out my prod again and let him see me turn it on. "So, Matt, that's what it's like to get force fucked!" I told him. "I could have done it myself: as you saw when I shot my cum all over your face, I've got a big dick, too. But I didn't want it up your dirty ass, and so I used the dildo instead. I've got some good pictures, Matt - pictures that will go up in the BDQ, and in the bar over the road, and out on the web. Do you want all the other draymen to see you with big black dildo up you, Matt? And for them to know that another man's cum has slimed all over your face? So just lie the quietly until I've gone, and let there be no thought of you taking revenge tomorrow - you touch me, and the stuff will be where everyone can see it."

I turned and walked out of the door, and went along the corridor to tell Jon all about it. He was actually quite worried, as he said that Matt couldn't be trusted to leave me alone and that he thought I was now very at much at risk of a really serious beating. But I thought that I could take care of myself, and wasn't worried. I went back through the salve barns to make sure my slaves were OK, and wished them a cheery good night as I was in a good mood now, but as I went past Matt's slaves I also took a look in, and it was horrible! I don't think they had had clean straw for weeks, as it smelt rank and unwholesome, and they were just sitting there looking really miserable. They're not big, tough guys like mine as Matt didn't care what he was given, and they were an odd mixture of sizes and shapes. He also dressed them in shorts on the streets, as the company paid a "laundry allowance" for this, and the more I looked, the more it was obvious that Matt claimed the money, but never had their shorts laundered as they were all filthy and tattered. I really felt sorry for one slave in particular who was just sitting there with his back against the rear wall, his head resting on his drawn-up knees as if he was trying to comfort himself. I ordered the slaves to their feet, and as they did so this one slave seemed to have difficulty in rising, so I shouted at him to get a move on and one of the others called out "Please allow him more time, sir, as his collar hurts so much... Please don't cane him, sir...."

I called this slave to me and was horrified at what I saw - there must have been a rough place on the base of his collar as his neck was covered in sores, some of which were bloody, some weeping pus, and some which were covered in thick scabs. The collar must have been doing this for weeks, and how could Matt not have known as it was obviously affecting the slave's performance if it was so painful that he couldn't move quickly? I then noticed that a lot of the slaves were scratching themselves, and especially their pubes, and it occurred to me that there must be fleas, or even lice, in these filthy conditions! It was absolutely disgraceful, wasting the company resources like this, and I flipped open my cell and called to Jon to come down.

We ordered the slaves to strip, and the damage to their bodies was dreadful as there were cane stripes and whip marks all over them, not just on those areas where it's "safe" to cane a slave, such as the butt and thighs. Jon pulled on a pair of rubber gloves and started to look critically at the slaves' pubes and said quietly one word "Crabs!". The slaves were very thin, too, almost emaciated, and we wondered why as there was always enough food in the feeder to keep the slaves healthy and in good condition. Jon asked them when they were last fed, and one slave dared to say that Master Matt had given them breakfast, but was "as usual" punishing them for not working hard enough by withholding their dinner. I tell you, Stu, it was a complete disgrace: the sores, the filthy conditions giving rise to the crabs, and letting the slaves starve - how on earth was Matt supposed to get them to give the effort they needed to the Company? And he was certainly misusing our valuable assets. I turned to Jon and said "Fire him!", and when Jon started to argue as he quite liked Matt "as a person", even though "he clearly had a few work-related problems", I almost lost my temper with him, and told him that if he didn't fire Matt there and then, I'd tell dad about the very lax state at the depot!

We simmered down, though, and as we worked away together to try to recover the slaves, he did begin to realise that Matt had to go - he was just so fucking idle, so mad keen to get over to the pub, that he neglected his slaves, which were his responsibility. Then there was the issue of defrauding the company - he must be claiming "laundry allowance" for the slaves' shorts but clearly it wasn't being done: apart from anything else, the sight of these dirty creatures on the streets would not be a good advertisement for our company. With this many examples of his unsatisfactory performance, he could not, after all, sue us for wrongful dismissal!

The first thing I did was to fetch a couple of feeders over and we had the slaves kneel so that we could pump some food into them - a couple of complete doses each (you can't give them more, as it's so concentrated that it would be bad for them). Jon then ordered them to clear away their filthy straw (they'd even soiled it, as presumably Matt had not got them trained properly to only crap when they were in the showers), and to scrub out their cage with disinfectant before laying down fresh straw from the barn. Their shorts had to go, of course, and we then took them off to the showers, but as they came out they had to be clipped and shaved: Jon roused one of the slave "grooms" we keep to do things like this, and he clipped off all their body hair, and then shaved away the stubble. Jon told me that the only way you can really get rid of "crabs" - pubic lice - if you don't want a long programme of special shampoos and stuff is just to get rid of the nesting places, so all these slaves' hair just had to go.

You always think I'm "cruel" to slaves, Stu, so you'd have been proud of me then. The slave with all the sores looked so young and vulnerable as he knelt there in front of me, now more naked than he'd ever been before as he'd lost every trace of his hair. He was only about our age anyway, I'd guess, and with more of your taller, lanky build than mine, but he was so painfully thin that I could clearly see all his ribs outlined through his skin. I went to examine the sores, and he whimpered softly as I moved the collar and felt for the rough patch. Then, as I tried to calm him and reassure him, I asked him what his number was, and he said "Chad, sir. Master Matt doesn't give us numbers, but lets us use our own names." I fetched a file from over in the workshops, and as I gently filed away at the rough place, I asked him more about himself. Incredibly, Stu, he'd gone into the northern army at seventeen and was barely out of training before they'd sent him down to fight us! So he was just like us - at some point he'd have been listening to the same music, going to the same movies, learning the same stuff at school - but now he was a naked slave kneeling at my feet, and he'd be a slave for the rest of our lives. If the war had gone differently, Stu, it could have been us kneeling like that in front of some northerner! Once his collar was smooth, I rubbed salve into his wounds and disinfectant - he cried out as that really stung him - and as I worked away he seemed to grow in confidence as he looked up at me as my fingers massaged his neck. He said "Sir, please, sir, could you call my folks in Philadelphia? They'd take a collect call, sir, as they must be worried sick about me - I never got a chance to tell them I was captured, and dad, in particular, will be so worried as I'm his only son, and....". I had to stop him, Stu, as I didn't want to hear more about how similar we were - I mean, I might have to discipline this slave soon, and you can't afford to be too close to them. You know what they say.... in the words of the old saying "You can't be friends with a slave". It was the same with the southern guy, four, who had tried begging me to call his wife and tell her he was alive, as he'd left her with two small kids. I'd had to explain to him, as I now explained to Chad, that he was now a slave, and slaves don't have families! And even if their loved ones knew where they were, there was nothing they could do about it as a slave was a slave for life, with no possibility of being free again. In fact, in law, all sorts of stuff like marriages are automatically dissolved as the slave is of course not a real person and only people can marry, inherit money from their fathers, and so on. Still, he was good to look at, even in his pathetic state. And if I closed my eyes as I massaged the stuff into him, I could almost imagine it was you. Steve.

Steve: So, not content with fucking slaves, you're going into the BDSM scene too, are you? Tying up, leather dildos, shaving..... whatever next? I'm expecting an e-mail from you any day now telling me you've bought one of those female slaves - I know they're high priced as they're relatively rare as there were so few women in the army, but then, your dad can afford it! Perhaps you can share her with him? Look, I know it feels good to take revenge, but remember what the good book says "Vengeance is mine, sayeth the lord". I'm surprised you feel so passionately about these slaves - one minute you say they're just like animals, so they can be fucked and whipped and so on, and the next minute you're feeling sorry for them as they're dirty, lice-ridden, starving, and covered in sores, because their drayman doesn't take proper care of them! It strikes me you're a bit inconsistent, Steve: when it suits you, you say they're animals as you feel it's not right to fuck a man against his will (it's called rape - remember?). But then the next minute it's Steve the caring one, outraged that these "animals" are not being treated properly. Doesn't this strike you as odd? Stu.

Stu: Please.... No more of this! You almost made me vomit into the PC! I mean, even suggesting that I might fuck a woman. And as for sharing with dad - ugh! That great fat belly of his.... I can hardly imagine he could even mount a woman, let alone fuck her. But perhaps it mightn't be so bad - a lot of those women soldiers are really "butch" and if I took them up the ass it can't be all that different, can it? Still, who needs it, when there's enough proper sex to be had any time I want it, with my slaves.

And my attitude to the slaves isn't at all inconsistent - they are animals, and they are there to be used - used for work (when they need "encouraging" to give of their best), and used for sex, if I choose. And it's not "compassion" that makes me furious at the way Matt treated his gang, it's the waste of money involved! These slaves are really expensive, you know. There's a lot of the company's money tied up in them, and, really, that's going to be my money one day. Of course I'm furious when I see something that belongs to me being mistreated and devalued. I hope that clears it up, once and for all.

Anyway, let me tell you what happened next. Jon called Matt in the following morning and fired him. The bully argued and shouted, but Jon handed him a pile of expense claims where he'd put in for laundry for the slave shorts, and said he'd call the cops if Matt didn't clear out. And he let Matt "notice" that elsewhere on his desk there was one of the photos I'd taken of Matt with the dildo sticking out of his ass, and his face covered in cum where you could just see the last inch of my dick, which had clearly deposited the cum over him! Matt got the hint, that he'd be ridiculed by all the other draymen if he tried to stay, and stormed out. That left his team of slaves and, initially at least, Jon decided to rest them for a day, and then put them into the "pool" of spare slaves that we can use to back-fill a team if one of the regular slaves in that team is injured. I happened to be passing on my way to get two and the rest of my boys, as a driver came out to lead them away. Young Chad was standing there, looking really pleased to be let off work, as were the others. But I had an idea, and told the guard to take the other seven away, and to lead Chad over to my dray and tell him to wait.

When I'd got all the other eight in position on the pulling pole and we went off to load up, I told Chad to watch carefully as the warehouse slaves loaded all the packages. I've told you how they load them in "delivery route" sequence except for the large or bulky ones, and this always causes problems as the stuff gets out of sequence and sometimes we really have to search for a package, and that holds everything up. So I asked Chad if he could read, and he snapped back that if it wasn't for the war he'd be in college (like you, Stu!). I had to strike at him with the tawse for using that tone, of course, and then I gave him the loading manifest. I told him that his job was to ride on the back and sort the packages as we went along, so that the right one would always be to hand whenever we stopped. I tapped my cane with my hand as I reminded him that I wanted this done properly, and that I wouldn't tolerate delays as this was his sole task today.

The other slaves looked mildly rebellious as they saw they were going to have to pull the weight of another slave as well as the loaded dray, but this is where two is so good - within seconds he'd reminded them that it was no good bitching and arguing about it, as it was my decision, and they'd just got to get on with it and make the best of it. And, I have to say, it was another one of those strokes of innovative genius on my part - without any delays at each delivery point, we got back to the depot an hour earlier than expected. I looked at my eight sweating slaves and pointed out they had another hour of relaxation now, and I could see them nodding - so maybe they understood that my scheme wasn't so terrible after all. But who cares what they think? Mind you, I told two that I thought that Chad needed exercising, as although he'd been clambering around on the dray all day, that was hardly sufficient. So when I took them over to the cage and fed them, I put all eight of them in it as usual, then pushed Chad in as well before locking the gate for the night. Two at once cleared space in the middle of them all - not easy, given the size of the cage, and there were now nine of them in there and not eight, remember - and began to bark orders for Chad to run on the spot, then do "jumping jacks", then push-ups. At first Chad tried to simply ignore two and not do it, but two is of course six inches taller and at least fifty pounds of pure muscle heavier than Chad. After a couple of attempts to reason with him, two bent down, grabbed Chad and put him over his knee, and gave him four big slaps on the butt. Chad squealed, I can tell you, but when he saw all the other slaves were laughing he realised that two had not hurt him all that much, and that he'd better do as he was told in case two really turned nasty. I went home feeling really pleased with progress. Steve.

Steve: OK, so the odious Matt has gone. But you've thrown this poor kid, the one who looks like me, in with these eight big horny men and locked them in overnight together? I thought you told me that there was only just room for the eight to sleep as it was, as it was a deliberate policy, to help with "bonding". And now you've added a ninth? I think I can feel my ass beginning to ache just at the thought of it! I suppose you're expecting these eight big guys to fuck the kid - they're all taller, more powerful, older.... What chance does he have? Psychologists might say that you're doing "transference" - you really want to be in there yourself, being ravished by these guys! Or that you secretly want to ravish me, and you're living out a fantasy by having eight big bucks doing it to a guy who looks a lot like me! It's all a bit "deep", Steve.... Or were you just trying to reward your slaves for a job well done by giving them some tender young chicken (I believe the phrase is, in the circles in which you move!)?. Stu.

Stu: Firstly, I don't need to reward slaves. Slaves just do as they're told. When will you get this simple idea into your thick skull, college boy? Hmmm.... Have you switched from English Lit and poetry to psychology 101? Transference, indeed! You must know you're spouting a load of rubbish: I've never secretly wanted to ravish you - I've always been perfectly open and frank about it! It's only you who always stopped it getting interesting after I'd finally got you to see how much more fun jerking off together, rather than separately, was. No, I put the ninth slave, Chad, in there as I want him to become part of the team, a full part of the team. And I also want him to look good - a bit more muscle is always pleasing to the eye. And, anyway, what makes you think that he might get "ravished"? A lot of nineteen year olds are perfectly capable of taking charge and "ravishing" older guys, you know, even if they're bigger, stronger, etc. It all depends on who likes to give, and who likes to take, dick.

Anyway, the following morning when I went down to the cage it was good to see that two had protected Chad all night - the kid was spooned up against two, and two had his arm wrapped protectively around him. I woke them all up and had them kneel, then told them I wanted to see them all jerk off (I'd sort of got out of the habit of this, as I generally allowed them to fuck and stuff at night). All my eight at once started, of course, but a look of almost pure horror went across Chad's face! He looked a bit like you, Stu, that night when I suggested that after we'd got used to jerking off together, we might go on to something a bit more adult! He looked along the line of slaves and saw all their dicks sticking out and the hands in motion, and very reluctantly, very slowly, he began to do the same. They all make a lot of noise, actually - as they get near the edge they start moaning and grunting and crying out (I'd thought about ordering them to be silent, but it seems a pity to spoil one of the few bits of pleasure they have, and, actually, it's anyway quite a turn-on to have all these guys grunting away as their seed shoots out), and it didn't take long before Chad was the same: his head was thrown back and his back was arched, and his dick was really good when erect - nice and smooth, without any of those thick veins some guys have. They all shoot at different times, of course, and Chad was one of the first to fire, in spite of his embarrassment: it wasn't just the fact that he had to do this very "private" thing in public now, but he must have seen that his own body was so different from all the others around him - they were tall, muscular, tanned, and nicely trimmed, whereas he was shorter, thin, had stark white thighs and butt, and was completely hairless.

Still, when I allowed them all to stand up, he seemed to have the same type of smile on his face that all the others did, so I guess he enjoyed it. I called him out of the line then, and had him bend backwards over a "horse" so that his dick was at a convenient height for me to work with. I stretched his dick and balls away from his body - as gently as I could - and snapped one of the steel rings around, at the root, locking it shut with the special key. He now had the same sort of cinch ring as the others, except it was much more visible as there was no pubic hair to conceal it. He looked worried, and when I gave the order to march out to the dray, he looked around for his shorts: two evidently guessed what I meant to do, though, as he nudged Chad and made him jog out with the rest, and Chad then had to work away naked as the packages were all loaded. It was only as the dray approached the gates of the depot that he dared to lean forward and said to me "Please, sir, can I put my shorts on now?" and I had to give him the little lecture I'd given all the others about how he didn't need them, as his slave collar was absolutely sufficient. He looked so young and innocent with his thin white body, entirely devoid of hair, and as we went through the gates and out on to the highway he tried in vain to cover himself with his hands.

Today I tried an even more daring strategy for improving efficiency - instead of having Chad just sort the packages so we had short delivery stops, when those packages were very small I had him jump down from the dray, go to deliver them himself and then run to catch us up - we didn't stop at all. He seemed to hate it - well, think about it, Stu: a guy of our age, having to run naked (and more than that - remember, he was completely hairless) to talk to people as he got receipts signed for and so on, and then having to run at high speed with his dick bobbing up and down as he chased after the dray! But that's not the point, is it? The fact of the matter is that we achieved record delivery times, and even though all the slaves were bone tired (the eight on the dray were used to having short breaks in the stops, and Chad was of course running most of the time), it was a huge increase in efficiency. That night I rewarded them all with a couple of slave treats, and declared it another "free sex" night - not that I think most of them were in the mood, as their limbs all ached a lot. Steve.

Steve: Great news! I proposed to Inga last night, and she accepted. We're planning to get married in the Fall, from our house, as my mom and dad and all the family don't want to travel to Sweden - Inga's folks are happy to come here, though. Will you be my "best man", as Inga calls it - you know: organise the stag night, get me to the church on time, make sure I have the ring, look after the bridesmaids, make a funny speech at the reception.... and all that sort of stuff? But seriously, though, Steve: remember, dad's a respected pastor, and we have a position to maintain in society. So no stripping me naked at the stag night, no risky jokes at the reception.... This is serious, Steve: I want to spend the rest of my life with her, and I don't want it all to start badly. Stu.

Stu: Of course I will! If you hadn't chosen me I'd never have spoken to you again. And I promise not to strip you at the stag night - but if you're very drunk, I might just jerk you off as we used to! Speaking of which, why don't you come down for the weekend, and let's just be close, and talk, and laugh, and have "fun" just as we used to, before you went away? Now that you're fucking women it doesn't mean that you can't also have a little recreational sex with your oldest buddy. A lot of married guys do, so it must be OK for engaged ones, too. Steve.

Steve: I love Inga, I told you that. I couldn't have sex with another guy when I'm in love with her. I don't care what other men do - this one isn't going to. And you're making a false assumption: we're not "fucking" as you so inelegantly put it. We're saving each other for our wedding night. Stu.

Stu: You can't be serious! How on earth can you even think about marrying her when you haven't fucked her? What's the matter? Are you afraid, or something? It certainly can't be that you're ashamed of that dick of yours, or your body - both very desirable, believe me, speaking as one who has a keen appreciation of the male form. Come on home, buddy, and let's get this sorted - we're close enough that you can tell me what's wrong, and I promise not to laugh! If it's your lack of experience you're worried about, we can just get two or one of the other formerly married slaves to tell you what to do and how to do it! I'm told that providing you do it "doggy fashion" a nice ass isn't all that different from some woman's cunt, so we could get one of the slaves to tell you about it, then you could practice on him, then he could critique it. Steve.

Steve: Look, Steve, I don't suppose you can understand this, but the Lord tells us in the bible that marriage is a sacred trust, and that it's wrong to have sex outside marriage. So I'm remaining chaste until after the ceremony. And as for the idea that I might fuck one of your slaves, it's preposterous - that's certainly a sin, "for one man to lie with another"! So let's drop this one, shall we? I'll get home as soon as I can for a weekend, but there won't be any fucking - not even any jerking off together. Look, I want us to stay friends, just as we always have been, but marriage changes everything and inevitably there will be some differences in the way we hang out and so on - for one thing, I expect Inga and I will ask you around to dinner, and stuff like that, and there won't be as many times when we are just alone together. But let's stay friends, OK? Stu.

Stu: Of course we'll stay friends. Even if I am a miserable sinner, in your eyes, for "lying with another man" - although as I mostly go with slaves now as most of the other guys are away at college, like you, I suppose that's OK as they're not men (no, don't respond, I'm only teasing!). Let me tell you about how things are going here in the boring old world of work, though.

Having the young slave Chad doing most of the deliveries then running to catch up with the dray was a real success, as we now could go back to the depot and load up again in the day as we'd saved so much time. The slaves all grumbled, of course, but a few gruff words from two, reinforced by a little light caning from me, soon restored them to their senses and made them properly respectful and obedient again. Chad soon put on a bit of muscle and ceased to look like a half-starved waif, but not so much that he looked as well developed as two and the others - well, at our age it's difficult, isn't it? However much you work out you tend to keep toned and fit, but unless you devote yourself to it full time you can't get those ridges of muscle on your belly, and bulging biceps, and so on - that seems to happen as you get more mature. He really does remind me of you, Stu - providing, that is, you've kept up going to the gym! Nice long legs, a butt that just calls out for fucking, and a dick that's just right for his body size hanging over nice low, swinging balls. And he's got cute eyes, too - the most astonishing piercing shade of blue, and nice white, even teeth. I suspect he's a virgin, too - when I'd initially inspected him his ass was so tight, and he squirmed so uncomfortably as I tried to push a finger in that I suspected that he'd never had proper sex - just like you, Stu! And since he'd been with my team, they'd kind of treated him as some sort of "mascot" - this much younger, slimmer, guy in amongst all those mature men - and they hadn't even tried to fuck him. He generally sleeps curled up around two, as if this gave him "protection" from the others, and, so far a I could see from scanning the security tapes, two had never even tried to take advantage of him. He did the "group" sex things of course, as he had no option but to obey me when I made them line up and jerk off together in the mornings (well, you can't have these naked slaves going through the streets dripping pre-cum, can you? It would send the wrong sort of messages to our customers. So the slaves needed "draining" occasionally, and getting them all to do it at one time is the easiest way of making sure all of them have done it).

I'd been over to the bar for a couple of beers with the other draymen - even though Matt had gone, the bar tender still served me as he valued the depot's business too much to bother about enforcing the law - and was walking back to the depot a bit unsteadily, when my dick went hard. I don't know why - we all get spontaneous erections, don't we? Even poets like you, who don't have sex....? It's part of being a young male! I was really aching by the time I'd got back as my dick rubbed against the material of my uniform shorts, and I was almost desperate to jerk off. I thought about putting one of the slaves on the "horse" and fucking him, and as my mind raced through the possibilities and was busy selecting which of the eight I'd have, I almost completely forgot Chad. But once I'd thought about him, it was impossible to get him out of my mind. I just knew that I was leaking pre-cum all over my shorts as I imagined his lovely tender butt pulled apart and my dick nudging at his virgin hole: it would be such a change from the big, hard muscles of the other slaves. And I might even be taking the cherry of a guy my own age - our age, I should say. Other than the bit of mutual jerking off we did together, I'd never had sex with a guy like us before, and the more I thought about it, the more this is what I knew I must do! My pace speeded up and my heart began to thud with the excitement in store for me, and my brain filled with the images of Chad's slim body on the horse, of the way he'd buck and scream as my dick went into him, and how it would feel afterwards to be lying on top of a fresh young body like his: it would be such a change to feel his body under mine and to have my thighs hard up against his almost smooth ones, rather than the tough curly hair on one of the other slaves.

I went into the slave barn, but when I got to the cage with the nine of them in it, I began to sweat with apprehension. I'd never had any problems before when I'd decided to fuck one of the slaves, but for some reason I suddenly began to worry that when my dick was having to force itself in to him, I might have one of those embarrassing failures as my dick went soft on me - it does happen occasionally to all of us, after all. And the more I thought about it, the more I knew it might happen, and then all the eight others watching me through the bars would start to laugh at me... And as I thought about that, my dick started to go soft!

A Boner Book

PART 9

Stu: I had to stop that last note to you as I broke out in a sweat as I thought about the shame of failing to perform in front of those eight big tough slaves - I'd lose all their respect, as I bet they had never done anything like that (or, if they had, it would have been in the privacy of their own bedrooms and they'd never tell their buddies about it). And then as my mind raced through what happened next, I got such a fucking erection that I just had to jerk off - and as you know (or perhaps you don't!) it's not a good idea to do that at the PC as if you shoot cum all over the keyboard it drips down inside and it's really gross!

Anyway, I had this terrible dilemma - I really wanted to take Chad's cherry and see what sex with a guy the same age was like. But I hated the idea of all the other slaves laughing at me if I failed! I mean, it's bad enough if you were just having sex with a guy in private and your erection failed, but to have it happen with an audience would be so shameful. I'd almost decided to give up the idea and just go and jerk off by myself, when it occurred to me that I could, after all, take

Chad to my room in the BDQ and fuck him privately. But then, he'd probably struggle as he wouldn't be there voluntarily, and I wasn't sure I could subdue him as he'd put on a fair bit of muscle and was almost certainly fitter and stronger than me! And what would happen if instead he decided to turn the tables and fuck me? I wasn't going to be raped again, as Matt had done, even though it might not be such a problem with Chad as his dick was more like yours, Stu, and not so very, very thick as Matt's had been. Still, if I subdued him in some way, that would be the ideal solution: I could always cuff him, I suppose, and I really didn't want to do that as I wanted to enjoy his body just as if he was like you and me. For that reason, too, I didn't really want to bring the portable horse into my room and fuck him on that - not even "buckaroo". I was still thinking it through when I got to the cage, and there they all were: I'd almost given up on the idea of fucking at all that night, but when I saw all their bodies together again, my enthusiasm was aroused (I mean, my dick was!). As soon as two saw me he shouted at the other slaves to stop what they were doing and line up neatly at the bars - he was like that, as he always thought that I wanted an "inspection", whereas I'd have been happy just to stand there and watch some of them fucking away. It seemed a shame, almost, to get them to stand there with their dicks jutting out in frustration, when they'd have rather carried on fucking and I'd have rather they did, too. But it's one of those disadvantages of an "officer" having a "sergeant" doing most of the control of the "troopers", I suppose.

Even though I'd been wavering, once I saw Chad standing there my resolution firmed (along with my dick, again!). I went and undid the cage and called two out, and stood there talking to him privately so that the other slaves should not hear. I told him I intended to take Chad's cherry that night, and asked him if he remembered how I'd taken his. When he nodded, I went on "So you know that being strapped on to the horse, with all the other guys watching, isn't really very great... Will you help me avoid that, two, by holding Chad down for me, if he needs it?". He shook his head, and my anger blazed for an instant. "You're a fucking slave, two, and don't forget it!", I snapped, "And if I tell you to do something, you do it, or suffer the consequences. I was telling you nicely that I wanted you to help me to take Chad's cherry, and you're refusing?". He looked a bit contrite, actually, as he mumbled "I'm sorry, sir, but... Well... You can't ask a guy to help you rape another one, sir...". I was really cross now, but I held my temper and told him that firstly, it wasn't rape, as Chad was a slave; secondly that he, two, was a slave, and had better do as he was ordered; and that thirdly, if he'd thought about it at all, instead of reacting stupidly, he'd see that he was helping Chad. "It's inevitable that I'm going to take his cherry, two", I finished, "So wouldn't it be better for Chad to have it happen with you there to help him get through it, rather than being strapped to the horse?" I didn't really give him time to react, and changed my tone to one of command, gave him the keys and told him to unlock the cage and get Chad out.

I strode across the yard towards the BDQ followed by two and Chad, and I noticed that two had his arm draped protectively around Chad's shoulders. Once up in my room I ordered two to stand quietly by the door and not do anything unless ordered, and then told Chad to stand close to me and undress me. He looked startled at first - as startled as you did, Stu, on that first time I told you to take my clothes off - and then we were naked together. If it wasn't for his all-over tan, the metal cock ring glinting in his pubes (which were re-growing), and his slave collar, we could have been two ordinary guys our age. I went to kiss him, but he pulled away, and I had to put out my arm and almost wrap it around him to pull us close. My dick was excited and I could feel it stabbing at him as he almost struggled to prevent our bodies touching, but then I realised he was the same way - his dick was poking at my belly, so I knew he must be at least a little turned on. With my other hand around the back of his head I pulled him closer and went to kiss him again, and he almost whispered "No, please.... I don't kiss guys...". "You mean you used not to kiss guys, Chad", I whispered back, not wanting to break the intimacy of the moment. "Now you do as you're told. Get your mouth open!".

He was so like you, Stu! Once my tongue was in his mouth, he just couldn't help responding, and I was soon running my hand up and down his back, and grabbing his butt, as I eagerly anticipated the delights to come as I carried on kissing him. Then I pushed him away, and said "On your knees, Chad!". He obeyed, as he was used to kneeling to be fed and when I ordered the slaves to jerk off, but now as I moved my dick towards his mouth, he started to lean backwards and whispered "No, please, no....". I ignored him, and pushed my dick at his mouth, and then when he didn't respond, I swung it and hit him on both cheeks, then trailed it around his face, holding the head under his nose so that he could smell me. With one hand behind his head I stepped forward a little and began to rub my pubes all over his face, so that his nose was plunged between my dick and balls, and then I relaxed a bit and again presented my dick to his mouth. "Open your mouth, you little fucker!", I said rather more forcibly now, and as he did, I pushed my dick in. You know how it is with inexperienced guys, Stu - or perhaps you don't, as we never got this far and I don't suppose you've been with anyone else since - but they don't remember to keep their teeth out of the way and so I had to tell him about that and how he'd be punished if they as such as scraped my sensitive skin again! I pushed in and out of him once or twice, but it wasn't all that much fun - he needed proper training, to be enthusiastic when sucking, and to learn not to gag when more than a couple of inches of my dick was in him. I didn't want to waste time with all that now, as if I decided to have sex with him regularly I could soon teach him to be properly responsive to me, so I told him to get up, and lie on the bed.

I lay beside him, and began to kiss him again, stroking his dick as I did so and hearing him moan. He was getting a bit turned on by me as we worked away, and he even began to respond to the kisses with his own tongue. His dick was so hard and throbbing in my hand that I knew the time was coming, so I rolled him over on to his back and began to help him jerk at himself, holding his hand as he worked away at it. I could see his eyes start to roll and his breathing to deepen as his climax approached, and then he shot, all over his belly. He wanted to stop, but the pressure of my hand kept him going and now he was thrashing his head form side to side and arching his back slightly as he moaned "No, no, no...." - he's one of those guys whose dick is evidently very, very sensitive after they've shot their first load: but it is important they learn to keep on milking themselves to get fully drained, I think. He lay there then, slightly panting, and I pulled myself close to him. "Right, Chad, now we've got some lube, it's time to get you ready...." He was so naive that he didn't understand, and looked puzzled. "You've got to get lubed up, Chad, as I'm going to fuck you.". He started to say "No, please...", but I had already covered my fingers in some of the cum which had conveniently pooled in his navel, and I was already scratching gently at his hole, pushing to gain entry. "NO, please, NO!" he almost shouted, and sat up, pushing at my hand to stop me.

"I was going to do this as if you were a buddy, Chad", I told him, "But as you seem determined to be stupid.... Get over here, two!" Two came over to the bed, and I told him to kneel between Chad's legs and get him stretched and lubed. Chad tried saying "No, no, no", again and again, but two, who had at first looked a bit rebellious before he saw the stern look I gave him, just went at it: the big guy knelt there and began to push his fingers up the young guy's ass, using his other hand on Chad's belly, to hold him down. Two didn't have to force Chad to lie there or anything - it was as if the insistent pressure of his hand, from a guy who was normally in charge of him, was sufficient. Chad was moaning now as two continued to work away, and when I saw that he'd got three fingers in so Chad must be ready, I gestured for him to move away and I now knelt between Chad's legs. I lifted one ankle and pushed it forward, telling Chad to grab hold of it, and then the other, so his ass was exposed to me - it was a great sight, the firm thigh and butt muscles holding the young skin taut, and the neat darker pink pucker waiting there, gleaming with the cum from its lubrication. I shuffled forward and positioned my dick head on it, and was about to push forward when Chad let go of his legs and tried to sit up, crying "No, no!". Once sitting, he kind of scooted away from me, up the bed, to rest against the headboard.

"I'm going to fuck you, Chad!", I told him. "Now lie down again, and let's have none of this nonsense!! Hew just sat there, shaking his head, defying me, and I began to worry that I was going to have to really punish him if I allowed this disobedience to go on any longer - remember, I wanted to enjoy this slave, not just do it as a matter of duty! I got up off the bed, then told two to lie there on his back and to put Chad between his legs. The big slave did as he was commanded, tugging at Chad so that he was sitting between two's open legs as two lay there. "Hold him back", I said to two, and "Keep his legs apart with yours", and, interestingly, Chad seemed to offer little resistance as two put an arm around his chest and pulled his body back so he was lying on two. There was a bit of grappling then as two kind of got his massive legs on top of Chad's so that Chad had to keep them apart, and finally I went and knelt there again.

It was kind of interesting, actually - having two there, visible underneath Chad's body seemed to add to the excitement I was feeling as I pushed my dick into him. It was absolutely amazing - well, it was tight, really tight, and his ass gripped my dick and sent waves of excitement through me. But to know that I was the first, and that this guy was utterly under my control now added to my excitement. He was moaning and groaning as you do when a dick bludgeons past the sensitive membranes of your sphincter, and then, as my excitement mounted and I started to lose control, thrusting faster and faster and harder and harder, Chad began to shout and almost scream. There was nothing he could do about it, of course, but he tried to, writhing and moving against the pressure of two's arms and legs holding him there as I moved as close to him as I could so that I could bury the entire length of my dick in him. I was so turned on, Stu, especially when I began to get that wonderful aching sensation in my nuts as they slammed against Chad's body. And then it was over - it only felt like a couple of minutes, but I think I was actually fucking for more like eight or nine before I shot a huge load up into him. I fell forward on to Chad then, feeling his hot, sweaty body against mine, and it wasn't clear to me whose heart was racing the fastest, or whose breathing was the most ragged.

I lay there for a couple of minutes, just enjoying that incredible feeling of closeness to another guy after you've fucked, even if he is a slave! Oh, I do wish we'd got that far, Stu!. Then I pulled out of him, and sat up. I nodded at them, to show two that he could let Chad sit up too, and Chad sat there just looking dazed. My dick was covered in cum and sweat, of course, so I got to my feet and went and stood by two's head as he lay there. "Open up, two", I said conversationally, "...and clean me up." I saw it then, Stu - a lock of defiance, only for a second or so, before two's good sense got the better of him and he began to lick at my dick to clean me. And I'm sure I saw something approaching contempt, too. Chad was watching all this, and when two had finished, I told him to go and lie face down with his belly on the bed and his feet on the floor. Chad seemed amazed as I sauntered across towards two with my cane, and brought it down hard, twice, once on each of his muscular ass cheeks. Two cried out with each stroke and his body tried to surge forward across the bed, as if to avoid me. But I only gave him those two strokes, and then I stood there, allowing my fingers to trace the bright red lines that had formed across two's butt.

"That's a lesson for you, Chad", I said quietly. "Two cleaned me off as instructed, but he wasn't enthusiastic! A slave needs to learn not only to obey, but to obey totally and completely. It's a privilege to have your master's dick offered to you, and two knows that. He should be setting you a good example, and because he only obeyed grudgingly, I had to punish him. Let's see if he does better this time...." I changed my tone, and said to two "Right, I've been doing all the work here. Now I'm going to lie and watch a little spectacle - fuck Chad for me, two. Good and hard. And with enthusiasm, please.... I don't want to have to punish Chad if I'm not turned on by seeing him fucked, if you understand me." I knew that two could take a caning, of course, so it was no use me threatening to punish him if he didn't fuck Chad "properly" - he didn't like the cane physically but could stand the pain, and it was more the humiliation for two that concerned him. But once he heard that I intended to cane Chad if two didn't perform well, that was different - two knew that it was inevitable that Chad would get fucked again, so he'd be intent on making sure that when it happened at least Chad wouldn't be punished afterwards.

I lay there propped up against the head board and played with my dick as two moved swiftly to obey me. He decided to take Chad doggy fashion, and soon had the lad kneeling on the bed, with his face pressed down into the mattress. Two was so sexually accomplished - he's physically superb, of course, but he has a way of controlling things, and even though Chad shouted, moaned and screamed as two's massive dick first penetrated him and then began to give him a hard, fast fucking, two was totally in command. He had one of his big hands on Chad's neck so he couldn't raise his shoulders, and with the other he alternated between pulling Chad's body back towards him as the fucking proceeded, and just letting it hang loosely by his side as he worked away.

When he'd finished, two pulled out and then just knelt there, his big detumescing dick hanging over Chad who was still lying on his face. He'd shouted and moaned as two had fucked him, but now he was silent and I called to him to come and lie by me. Slowly, he raised himself to his knees and then, not looking at two, he stretched himself out by my side. I threw one leg companionably over him, enjoying the feel of his dick on my thigh, and put out an arm to go under his head, so he could rest against my shoulder - I'd often wished that you and me could have been together like that, Stu, but after we'd jerked off, it was always as if you were somehow guilty about having enjoyed yourself and wanted just to get up and pull your shorts back on. Two continued to kneel there, and now he was looking at us.

"You OK?", I asked Chad, and he muttered "I guess so." I smiled at him, and gave him a gentle squeeze. "That was your first time, wasn't it? And now you've had two guys fucking you." He nodded a "yes", and I said casually "And I suppose you've never had sex....?" He looked surprised, as he muttered "Oh yes, sir. I had a girlfriend - well, several, actually.". I smiled again. "No, I mean proper sex, sex with another guy.". He was like you, Stu, it turns out: he'd had some jerking off with his buddies, but that was as far as it went as he'd started to fuck girls. Well, not like you, I suppose, as you're "saving yourself"!

Chad shook his head, and I saw that this was a way to further my control of him, and at the same time to make two understand that he was just something that I could use, as I wanted. I snapped at two to lie on the bed, at the end, so that he was facing me, with his feet on the ground. Then I almost pushed Chad away, saying "OK, now's your chance to find out what it's all about really - get and fuck two for me." Two had by this time rested his head on his crossed arms in an attitude of total relaxation, as he obviously thought that after holding Chad down for me, and then fucking him himself, his part in the night's proceedings were over. But now his head came up, and for an instant I thought he was going to protest - but all he did was flash me a look of almost pure hatred. He knew it was useless to argue, but clearly he didn't like what was about to happen to him. It was Chad who objected - he called out "No, please, sir, no - I can't do that."

"Why not?", I asked, and he blurted out a whole lot of stuff about respecting two, having two as his friend, two had protected him from the other slaves.... Until I said simply "Stop! All this is irrelevant, Chad. I've told you to fuck two, and you will. You're a slave, and slaves obey, and that's all there is to it. Now get down there, spread his butt, get yourself boned up, and in you go!" He just stood there, looking at me, saying "No, please, no.....", so I got up off the bed and crossed the room, very conscious that both slaves were watching my dick bob up and down as I did so - the excitement of the moment had made me spring a boner, of course.

Two more bright red stripes appeared across two's butt, each accompanied by a satisfying grunt from two to indicate that they were really hurting him and that he was trying to not show it. "I'll carry on caning two, shall I, Chad? I'll give him one stroke every minute until your body is covering his butt and I can't get at it.... Fuck him, or have him caned. It's your choice."

I ought to write a book about controlling slaves, Stu, as it's so easy once you get the hang of it! Before I could raise my cane again Chad was standing there, behind two, looking really nervous. I had to tell him to start jerking himself off to make him throw a boner - I can't imagine why, as I found the thought of this young guy about to fuck big, strong two so erotic that my own dick was almost shooting off all by itself! Then he had to be told to stand in-between two's legs and kick them apart a bit. He stabbed ineffectually at two's ass until I pointed out that with a deep, muscular "bubble" butt like two's you needed to pry it apart a bit with your hands to reveal the pucker. He was hopeless even then, though, and almost in desperation I went and stood behind him, took hold of his dick and positioned it right at two's entrance, and then pushed forward against Chad to make him go in! His dick started to bend a bit, and it needed some encouragement, so I moved away and slapped him hard on his butt, which seemed to do the trick - you know how it is: once you can get even a little bit of your dick head in, it's so much easier to make the rest follow. Oh no, I forgot, you don't know how it is, Stu! Well, it is.

I put my hand on his hips and pulled him backwards and forwards at first until he'd got the hang of it, but then, once the sensations took over, he seemed to be quite enjoying it as he gave two what I can only characterise as a "good hard fucking" - no finesse to it at all, just good, solid hard pounding with the whole length of his dick, his body making a most satisfactory slapping sound each time it hit two's butt.

When he'd finished, I wondered if I should complete two's humiliation by making him kneel and clean Chad's dick. I let two know it was within my power to do this by joking that Chad might now enjoy the feeling of two's big tongue around his dick and balls, but then said that I was in a hurry, so Chad should go into the bathroom and clean himself up. When he was in there I told two to come and lie next to me, and instead of curling up in his arm as might have been expected as he was so much bigger than I was, I deliberately stretched out my arm so that he had to cradle his head on it, and I threw my leg across his belly and dick, as he'd seen me do to Chad only a few minutes before. I knew that, subconsciously at least, I was relegating this big powerful man to the status of a much weaker nineteen year old. I reached across and tweaked two's big tit playfully as it lay conveniently close, and looked deep into his eyes. "I do worry about you, two", I said quietly, so that only he and I could hear. "Every time I think I have you properly tamed and that you truly understand that you're a slave, you do something stupid. I saw that look in your eyes when I ordered you to clean me up. And that's why I wanted to see what you would do when I ordered Chad to fuck you - you don't like taking dick, I know, and you never do from any of the other slaves. It was good for you that you did not deliberately disobey me physically, as I'd then have needed to have you flogged. But I saw the look in your eyes and it was one of pure hatred for me. That's not good enough, two. I don't only want your complete physical obedience to my orders, but you have to want to obey me, too. If you don't understand that, or can't implement it, I'm afraid that there will be a lot more trouble for you.". At that moment Chad came back, so I leaned over and kissed two affectionately, pleased that he responded as another man should, but then, as it was getting late, I got up, pulled on my clothes, and took them back to lock them in their cage for the night. At two went through the gate I said quietly "Make sure Chad gets fucked at least once more tonight - get four to do it, as he can't hide things from me very easily as he's just a simple country boy, and tomorrow morning it will be easy to tell if you've done as I've told you." Two kept his head down as he went in, so that I couldn't see his eyes: I knew he'd hate passing on that order to four, but what else could he do? Steve.

Steve: It's beginning to sound more like some porn movie! Three in a bed, changing partners, young men kissing older guys..... And I'm not sure that all this constant referral to Chad as "being like me" is helpful, Steve! You aren't going to get my mouth around your dick, or in my ass, either! And neither am I going to fuck guys' asses, however muscular or desirable you seem to think they are! It's amazing, really, how you and me can be such good buddies when our tastes are so dissimilar. Still, the good news is that I'm coming home next weekend - we're arriving on the afternoon train on Saturday, but only for a flying visit to really introduce Inga to mom and dad. I'm not sure that you and I will be able to get together for long, as we have to get back on Sunday as I have an early class on Monday morning. Stu.

Steve: That wasn't funny! When we came out of the station to get a cab and you were sitting there on that dray with all those slaves of yours....! And it wasn't very polite to insist I sat next to you on the seat with Inga on the outside - I think you don't like her, Steve, and you show it in all sorts of little ways like that: it would have been more polite to get her to sit in the middle so you could talk to her easily. I'm not surprised she didn't want to spend time with you, as you were radiating disapproval, even though you were, ostensibly, playing the part of the ultra-polite southern gentleman! And you know she objects to slavery, so why did you keep cracking that carriage whip of yours over the butts of those unfortunate slaves? They seemed to be working hard enough to me. And yes I know my dad's attitudes to all of this are ambivalent, to say the least - he's a pastor and he keeps preaching about freedom and treating all men as equals, and Inga respects all of that. So it was quite unnecessary to keep asking me if the slaves working in the fields as we got closer to our house were all ours, or just hired in from a contractor to get in the harvest. You know perfectly well that dad owns about a hundred, and the reason why: he's "saving" them from a cruel life elsewhere, as he's a benevolent owner. Stu.

Stu: If he's so benevolent, why do his guards all carry whips? And why doesn't he even allow them a shred of clothing? It's for the same reasons my slaves work naked: it's a waste, to buy slaves clothes, clothes that have to be laundered and so on; and when they're naked, it's easier for the whip to get at their sensitive parts. And you need a whip to keep them working!

And I think you don't appreciate the trouble I went to, to collect you from the train station: it was Saturday afternoon, and the slaves are expecting to rest! They really resented it when we got back to the depot on Saturday lunchtime and then I made them clean and polish the dray, and shower and shave themselves, and then rub in slave oil to make their pelts really shine, just so I could act like a taxicab! They're so fucking ungrateful - just because I made them do a couple of hours of extra work, work that's not hard, after all, compared to pulling a full dray, they were all sullen and resentful. They forget the number of Sundays I've given up for them, so I can take them to the park! And that's why I was using the carriage whip a lot, too - they knew I knew they were resentful, and therefore I needed to reinforce to them that I won't tolerate such attitudes in my slaves.

And I wanted to sit next to you, Stu, to catch up. Inga and I don't have anything to say much to each other. And when we do speak, it's only to argue - she doesn't agree with slavery, and that's OK, but it's not OK to compare her fiancee's best buddy to some sort of nineteenth century sadistic villain. I keep explaining that the ownership and management of slaves these days is soundly based on good management theory, but she just won't see that. And then she keeps trying to tell me that "the good lord will forgive me if I repent". Well, I don't need to be forgiven, as I haven't done anything wrong.. So what should I repent of? She said it was cruel of me to keep young Chad running along by the side of the others, for example, and I tried to point out that he likes being with the others! If I locked him in the cage on Saturday afternoon as he had no real role, but took all the others out, he'd have hated it. And then she said that it was cruel to keep him as a slave in the first place, and she didn't really listen at all when I told her how I'd saved him from a really cruel driver, Matt, and how being on the drays was a whole lot better than, for example, being chained to a factory bench, or down the mines.

I know you said you'd invite me to dinner and stuff once you were married, but I think the conversation around the table is either going to be non-existent, or pretty fiery!

Still, Inga's remarks about Chad did get me thinking, and perhaps I was being a bit unkind to him. After a few nights of being used by the other guys after I'd taken his cherry, he'd really felt much more part of the team and no longer a bit of an outsider. And when we were talking in a quiet moment one day, two even told me that Chad had fucked one of the "bottoms" in the crew - and had even joined in the laughter when the others saw him doing it and told him that his skinny ass was pretty funny as it pumped away (well skinny by their standards. I think it's pretty nice!). I remembered all of this, and decided to make him feel a lot more wanted, so yesterday I lashed them on a bit to build up some more slack in our schedule, then made a bit of a diversion to go down Eighteenth Street - you remember, that area that was so daring when we were both fourteen, and trying to buy the sexy magazines and stuff? It's still very seedy, but there's a tattoo parlour down there and I took Chad in. When we came out, the slaves all cheered when they saw the giant "9" on his back - that's real team-building for you, and it shows you just how good a manager I am. Steve.

Steve: We're coming back next weekend, too. And this time, PLEASE, old buddy, don't meet us at the station! What time do you finish work, and we'll collect you at the depot, and all go out to dinner together? But look, Steve, watch it, please, for my sake! I know you can get even more mischievous with a couple of drinks inside you (dad's promised to talk to the restaurant and there won't be any problem with getting a bottle of wine).... But Inga doesn't drink at all and takes a bit of a dim view of it at the best of times - if you get half cut and start arguing with her about slavery, or god, or whatever, it will make it hard for me. Stu.

Stu: Pick me up at seven. I'll have time to go over to the bar then and have a drink first - god knows, it sounds as if I'll need one, as it might be a grim evening with you and me sharing a bottle of wine and Inga sipping lemonade! You and I need to go on one of those "drunks" we used to, and have a bit of fun. But I'll even shower, and change into "civvies", so she isn't even reminded of my work by my uniform (although she'll be deprived of the pleasure of seeing my nice hard butt, and dick, through my shorts - I thought you were looking just a tad fatter last week, Stu - all that sitting down isn't good or you, and you need a good physical job, like mine, with plenty of sex). See you on Friday. Steve.

Steve: Bastard! I still can't type. Stu.

Stu: So, let's get the facts straight now, as I don't want to be arguing about it with you in forty years time still. Firstly, It was your fault for going off to buy her flowers or whatever, and sending her on alone to the depot. If you'd stuck close to her, none of it would have happened. Secondly, I didn't offer to show her the slaves. She practically DEMANDED to be taken to see "the dreadful conditions in which you keep these unfortunate wretches" or some such crap. They're not dreadful conditions, as they all get clean straw, they're well fed, there's enough water, hot showers, more sex than they'll ever need.... And they're not "unfortunate", either! If they hadn't joined the army, and then hadn't taken place in an illegal invasion of the south, they wouldn't be slaves at all - it's their own fault.

I took her to my slaves, obviously, as I'm proud of them and I think they represent the best aspects of the system. Although they were all tired, Friday night is a traditional "relaxation" night, and when we got there a few of them were fucking, and nine (Chad) and four were lying together, arms wrapped around each other, laughing and just jerking each other off. Two saw me coming and went to tell them all to "present" in a line at the bars, but as it was Friday and I'm pretty considerate, I signed to him to leave them all be. Just as we got there, one, who was buried up to the hilt in seven's ass, gave a great shout as he shot his load, and the two of them collapsed on to each other in that real affectionate passion you get after really great sex (as you might be lucky enough to discover one day, Stu!). Inga just said "It's absolutely disgusting!", and, of course, I asked her why. And then she and I had a bit of an argument, which I won't bore you with again, about firstly, they were slaves, so it wasn't as if men were having sex publicly (which even I disagree with!); and that secondly, even though it was two males, that was perfectly OK as the only reason anyone ever thought it might even be wrong was because of all that crap in the bible - and I think I did perhaps refer to the whole thing as being so full of shit anyway, that who cares what it said! But then she saw nine and four just jerking off, and started in again about it all. "And he's only a boy...", she finished with.

So I told her! Nine was nineteen, the same as you and me. And he was old enough to make up his own mind about sex. And, anyway, he wasn't doing much, just a bit of mutual jerking off, and all men did that at that age with their buddies - well, most of them had moved on to fucking, actually, as the mutual jerking off stage is from about fourteen to seventeen! She said that "her Stu" (she was starting to own you already, old buddy) would never do anything like that, and I just laughed. So she demanded to know why, and I told her - told her that you and I of course used to jerk off together - what did she expect?

We were both red-blooded guys with a lot of male hormones. Every guy I know in our set was doing the same, as it's perfectly natural to want to play with another guy, especially after a football match or something. But I assured her that you'd never done anything more than that, and that you were "saving" yourself for the wedding night.... So there was no real problem.

She went very silent, and ran out. And you know the rest. Or perhaps you don't! I gather you met her on the street, and she asked you if you and I had jerked off together, and as you don't believe in lying you told her the truth.... And she stormed off to the train station! You were fucking rude, and almost violent, when you came up to my room, Stu, and you were ranting and raving about me "betraying" you and all that crap. You could just have lied, Stu, and said that we'd never jerked off - she'd have thought it was me who was lying, to deliberately try to upset her! So it's more your fault than mine - to me it's perfectly obvious that two teenage buddies will have a bit of casual sex, and I can't see why bigots like her object at all. That's what almost all men do, after all, and it just shows how stupid she is that she didn't recognise that. It's just as well I had that bottle of bourbon in my room, and you did calm down after a couple of drinks. And then we started to laugh a bit, and then we went out to the restaurant and had not one, but two bottles of wine.... By the time we got to that dance place you were pretty far gone, but we both went onto the floor, and you met that girl - well, I tried to look after you, but you would insist on calling that cab yourself and going off in it with her. I did try, really. For one thing, I thought that with so much booze inside you I might have had to undress you.... And who knows where that would have led, so I was really motivated to get you home! But you did insist, and you are old enough to make your own decisions. So I staggered back to the BDQ alone, and I couldn't then get it up as I'd drunk so much. And the next day my head felt as if it was in a vice and my guts were churning and I could barely crawl out of bed. So I didn't catch up with you. So what happened next, old buddy? Steve.

Steve: What happened next? Mary-Lou happened! A real southern girl. All demure on the outside, but dynamite inside. I think you must have been feeling guilty or something and drank too much deliberately, as I wasn't nearly as bad as you. In fact, I was dreading having to carry you home and having you puke up all over me again as you did that once when we were fourteen! So when Mary-Lou said she wanted to go home I was the perfect southern gentleman, and took her. To tell you the truth, Steve, I was shit scared as although I've done all the kissing and petting stuff, I've never really done "it". And it was obvious that Mary-Lou knew that there was only one proper way to end an evening. But once we were in bed together naked, it didn't matter at all - it all seemed perfectly natural. Hey, Steve, I'm no longer a virgin! And you're right, old buddy - there's NOTHING as good as sex, and all that waiting stuff is just pure crap. Why wait for something that gets worse as you get older? Guys are at their horniest at sixteen, and even at our age we're starting to go downhill. I almost missed the train back to Atlanta on Sunday. And Mary-Lou's coming here next weekend - I can't wait to see the other guys' eyes pop out on stalks when they see this classy lady that I've got. Stu.

Stu: Ah well, that sounds as if I've lost the chance to have proper sex with you then - at least until you've been married a couple of years. That's when a lot of guys start to get bored, and regret what they've never had - proper sex, with another guy. But I'll keep waiting, Stu. You are coming back in three weeks time, aren't you? It's the County fair, and I'm entering. Steve.

Steve: Entering? As what? Isn't it for cattle and such like? Are you putting on one of those cow skins, like you see in comedy shows? Stu.

Stu: Yes, cattle and such. And a year ago they put in new classes, for slaves. They're things like "most obedient slave" where you have to get your slave to do things when he's blindfolded, responding only to your spoken orders, and "best confirmation" - that's a technical term they use in livestock judging that means the carcass is in good condition - not too muscled, but not fat, or anything. Then I think they have "best stud" or something, where the slaves have to be masturbated and the semen is judged on quality, colour, number of sperm per millilitre -

and of course quantity - and so on. But I'm entering my dray in the "slave-pulled vehicles" class - you usually get pony traps and so on, but Jon agrees with me that it would be excellent publicity for us if we win as our dray has the company name all over it. But it will be a lot of hard work, and the slaves will hate it. In fact I'm just typing this to you before I kick the whole thing off, and I'm expecting a difficult time. I'll write again this evening. Steve.

PART 10

Stu: Well I didn't manage to write to you, did I? A couple of days have gone by, and there's still trouble! I'd cecided that the way to win was to have an entry that's so much better than any of the pony traps that they just have to give me the prize, and that the way to do this was to have all nine of them identical - well, eight near clones, and nine as some sort of "extra" but on the same theme. The problem is that although they're all basically similar in body size and shape, they've all got different coloured hair and different amounts of body hair and so on. And, of course, two and a couple of the others still have their 'skins whereas the rest are cut. It seemed sensible to have the three of them 'skinned, therefore, and I'd arranged for the veterinarian to come in and do it.

When two heard about it he went berserk, and stood there in the cage shaking at the bars and calling me all sorts of foul names. It's just as well it didn't happen when he was out of the cage, as otherwise he might have actually attacked me! The only thing to do was to reach in and stun him, and whilst he was unconscious to cuff his wrists to his collar, and muzzle him. I really don't understand what all the fuss was about, as it's not a serious operation - it's not as if I was taking one of his kidneys for a dialysis patient, or some of the other stuff they use slaves for now. His dick would still function - function better, in my opinion, afterwards. And he'd save time in the shower in the morning without having to clean under that 'skin..... It's not at all painful, either - in fact, down at the auction rooms if you want your slave 'skinned they just do it on the spot, without even a mild anaesthetic. But I'd paid my own money to have the veterinarian to come in and do it "humanely", with a shot into the dick first, and it was only supposed to take three minutes each and so the day's work wouldn't be affected. But now with two stunned and muzzled, all that was upset.

I had to get two of the other slaves to hold two still as the veterinarian operated - we had him on a horse, with one sitting on his thighs and one on his chest, and then he basically couldn't move as the 'skin was neatly cut around and the stitches to hold the cut ends together were put in - well, not stitches as such, but some sort of small mini-staples which automatically dissolve in three days. The little tool the veterinarian used was really neat - just click, click, click and the job was done. He advised a plaster around the wound, but only for one day, and then it was all over. I kept the little ring of skin that was cut off, as I thought I might dry it and add it to that bead necklace you've seen me wearing when I'm aggressively casually dressed. The others weren't that much trouble, as they'd seen what I did to two, and just stood there with their dicks on a low table as he did them. But there was further delay, of course, as I had to punish two - I mean, I could hardly let him get away with that sort of behaviour in front of the other slaves.

I'd undone two's cuffs as he' d calmed down a bit, and I told him that I'd only take the muzzle out if he understood that there was to be no discussion on what had gone on - I ought to have kept him muzzled all day, of course, but I needed him to keep the others doing their proper jobs as we worked and so it was in my interests to have him able to speak. He nodded, although with a sour expression, and so I told him that I'd just added two more strokes to his punishment for that piece of dumb insolence. I ordered h m back on to the horse, but I decided to allow him to start to grow back the respect of the other slaves - who I don't think liked two's outburst - by not cuffing his wrists and ankles to the legs: he'd demonstrate that he was tough and could take the beating, and that he was obedient by standing there unshackled.

It takes a lot of physical effort to administer ten strokes of the cane, and by the time I'd done, I was pretty pissed off with two still. He'd stood there, just grunting as each blow hit, deliberately holding back his screams to "prove" his manhood to the others. And I was worried that the livid red stripes all across his butt now might not fade in time for the County Fair - I could hardly expect to win a prize with a slave who was so clearly disobedient that he needed that much punishment, could I? Still, it had to be done, and I have to say that for the rest of the day he was an example to them all, working even harder than usual, and taking control and really making my life easy. That night, though, I decided he still needed to be punished further, and so after all the others were fed and caged, I ordered him to come with me to my room in the BDQ. He stood there looking proud and defiant, his dick half erect as a result of the metal cock ring, and I said simply "You know what comes next, don't you, two? On your back, legs in the air, and hold your ankles...."

For an instant he looked as if he might be going to protest, but then he lay there as I'd ordered, and I took some time undressing and stroking my dick to erection. "This is going to hurt, two", I told him. "You're still resisting my authority, and that's got to stop. You're lucky to escape with a caning this morning, and now I'm going to fuck you, fuck you hard, and that striped ass will really feel it!". There' something special about fucking a man in that position anyway, as you can see the effect your dick is having by watching his face as you go in to him, and tonight I was rewarded by seeing how two desperately tried to control his features as he tried not to let me see that he was hating the fucking, and that it was hurting him a great deal: I had not bothered with stretching or lube of any kind, and the caning was already very sore without my body slamming into it all the time. I made no effort to be gentle and this was just a hard, fast, furious fuck, where I almost pulled right out on each stroke and then slammed back in. It was wild and exciting for me, then when I'd cum, I threw myself alongside two and lay there, exhausted, but almost laughing with happiness as I'd enjoyed it so much.

Two shifted uneasily alongside me, and I turned towards him and went to stroke his nipple, to show him I was no longer so cross with him. He almost drew away, and I felt my anger rising again. "Is something wrong, two", I almost snapped, and he muttered "No, sir. Not really."

"Not really? I think there's something very wrong, two! Your attitude! That outburst this morning, then you deliberately didn't cry out tonight, you didn't participate, and that takes away some of my enjoyment. You knew that, didn't you? Is that the way a slave ought to behave?". He turned his handsome face towards me and said simply "You had me 'skinned, sir! You took away my manhood. That's not right, sir. You shouldn't have done that...."

"You stupid fucking slave", I snapped back. "You've just shown me how wrong I've been to try to treat you well, to let you almost be a sergeant again, instead of just treating you like one of the other slaves. Something I ordered done to you is 'not right'? How can something I order for a slave not be right? And I didn't 'take away your manhood' - you're just as much of a man now as you ever were, it's just that you'll look neater and tidier, and more like the other slaves. I need you all to look alike, and as I can't grow foreskins back on the five of you who were already cut, the three of you with 'skins needed to lose them. It's as simple as that - you're all my slaves, and if I want you all to have a certain 'look', that's what will happen. And if you ever protest, or defy me like that again, it won't just be your 'skin that you lose - it will be your balls; and that will REALLY mean you lose your manhood! Is that clear, two? And if you want to remain as my 'sergeant', I want to see a complete change in your attitude: it's not enough for a responsible slave like that just to obey, he has to accept his owner's orders, and communicate that acceptance to the others. Is that all clear?"

He looked at me, and I could almost see him thinking. He could see that he ultimately couldn't win. And he did like being 'special'. He said quietly "Yes, sir", and then, without being ordered, half sat up, bent towards me, and started to clean my dick with that big sexy tongue of his. After he'd finished I was almost laughing as he'd kind of tickled me with his tongue, and he was smiling, too. I decided to do something I'd never done before and keep two with me all night. He was used to sleeping with other men of course, used to the way they move around and cry out in their sleep, but I wasn't and at first I found it hard to adjust to the solid warmth of him right next to me, and the sound of his breathing and the scent of his body.... But then he turned towards me and wrapped his arms around me and pulled me close to him, and I realised just how lucky nine was to have this fantastic man taking care of him like that. He put his arm under my head and generally moved our bodies until we were both comfortable. My face was so close to his I could feel his warm breath sighing over me, and I just felt very content, very safe.

I woke up at about three, and realised that two was still holding me, and that he was awake, lying there looking at my face. He saw me looking at him, and he just smiled quietly and then pulled me closer to him, so that our erect dicks pressed into each other. I drifted back into sleep, utterly contented. Steve.

Steve: Sex isn't just about fucking, you know. It sounds to me as if you had a kind of sexual experience with two after you'd fucked him. He sounds a really nice guy, to have you 'skin him, then beat the shit out of him, then rape him again (he didn't want to do it, did he?), and still be so gentle with you. I think you're falling for this slave. Take care. Stu.

Stu: There you go again! "A really nice guy", "rape".... He's a slave, and lost the chance to be a "really nice guy" when he was captured. And as I've explained before, you can't rape a slave. And no I'm not falling for him - "You can't be friends with a slave", remember? But what do you know about sex - come on, Stu, stop trying to give me advice on that score!

But anyway, our little night of passion did seem to have one effect - when we got back from the route tonight and I put the next part of my plan into affect, the moment some of the others started a rumble of complaint, he really laid into them, verbally and physically, to tell them to shut up and obey. Steve.

Steve: Don't leave me in suspense! What is the plan? Stu.

Stu: Oh, yes - I got so caught up in the execution of it that I forgot to mention it! The plan is to have all eight of the slaves to be "clones", as far as possible. Having the three of them 'skinned was the first step, and then I did the rest: I'd noticed that nine looked so totally different, so very young, so very vulnerable, when we'd had to shave off all his hair because of the crabs, and realised that if I did the same to the eight slaves, they'd be so much alike! Without a trace of hair below the eyebrows, the similarities between them would be even more pronounced. And, of course, without thatches of hair on some of their chests and bellies, you'd be able to see their superb musculature so very much better. So it all had to go, every scrap, and I had the "grooms" who normally did the clipping and shaving in for a long session.

As I said, there was a lot of grumbling and complaining once they realised what was going to happen to them, but two quelled it all and just said that if it was my orders, then they had no choice. And when it was all over, I think some of them quite liked it - I saw them preening themselves in front of one of the mirrors, admiring the way their definition was now so much more pronounced. I thought it showed them off to perfection, especially as the glint of their steel cock rings tended to draw the eye down to their genitals - which, as I've also told you, are pretty nice anyway (for those of us who have an eye for such things!). When the grooms started on the next and final phase, though, even two looked a bit rebellious, but when he saw me fingering my cane, he just nodded, smiled faintly, and brought the others into line again.

Look, it's no good having all these near-clones from the eyebrows down, when they all had such very different hair - some smooth, some a little coarse, some dark, some that sexy dirty blond... I'd thought of having their skulls shaved as well as their bodies, but I'm not sure I like to see men with that totally bald look. Some would say the differences were pretty minor, as I always had them kept closely cropped (which they seemed to like, anyway, as they were ex-marines and so on), but then I hit on the ideal solution: I had the grooms trim and shave their heads so that they just had a three inch strip left down the centre - a Mohican cut, I think they used to call it. But then I wanted them all dyed the same colour, and before you can do that you have to bleach all the natural colour out, and they hated standing there with that terrible smell of bleach hanging in the air as it did its work. I'd wondered whether I should have them all black, or all blond, but somehow there's a link between a guy's "natural" colour and his face and so on - or perhaps I was just imagining it, as I was so used to seeing them with their natural hair. Anyway, as a special touch, I had decided to have their hair dyed really dark green, the same colour as the paint on the dray! I thought it would really add that final touch, to see the dray and the slaves now so intimately a part of a set.

When I looked at them after it was all over it was somehow amazingly erotic - the eight big muscled men dicks semi-erect, with this big streak of dark green across their skulls - I'd even had some of that wax brushed into it, to make sure the hair stood upright, rather like those old Roman soldiers' helmets. And nine looked sensational, too - even though he's fleshed out generally and put on some muscle, he somehow maintained that air of vulnerability, the more so as he was contrasted with the others. You know, Stu, I think I might try shaving all my pubes off - it's a look that suits our body types. Have you ever thought about doing it? Steve.

Steve: Oh my god! You're turning into some sort of costume artist and hairdresser! Still, isn't hairdressing one of those jobs that men like you go in for? (Joke, joke - you know I'm not prejudiced against gay guys). But no, I haven't thought about shaving my pubes, although after reading a note from you some time ago about how shaved balls are so much better, I have been doing mine since. You're right, of course, that they feel so much smoother and silky and are so much nicer to stroke when you're jerking yourself off. And Mary-Lou, that first time we went to bed, was amazed that a red-blooded guy like me could show such consideration for his partner as to do that - she went down on me, Steve, before we began fucking seriously, and she said how nice it was not to end up with hairs trapped between her teeth! But I'm not sure the totally bare look would suit me - or you! We'll both see you tomorrow, for the fair. And I know I can rely on you not to break our confidences - Mary-Lou knows we jerked off, and she's OK about that as she knows all guys do it when they're growing up. But please don't say you know she goes down on me - it's another one of those things where "everyone" knows that women do that to guys, but you just don't talk about it. Stu.

Stu: Your secret's safe with me! But if you're happy to have Mary-Lou sucking your dick, why did you deny yourself the pleasure with me? We could have had so much more fun. And I'm told by those that have done both that a guy really does it SO much better than a woman - well, he would, wouldn't he, as he knows the effect he's causing.. Perhaps when it's "that time of the month", or she's travelling, we might pick up where we left off! You see I live in hope of having that body of yours next to mine again one day - but there's no hurry, I can wait!

Anyway I must go now as it's time to see to the slaves - I'm having them really clean the dray, and I mean really clean it: every tiny nook and cranny is being cleaned out, and they've got to give it five coats of polish tonight, to give it a real depth of shine. And finally they've got to give themselves the first coat of slave oil - I want their pelts with that deep, healthy glow tomorrow, and a good soaking tonight that has time to go into the skin will make sure that tomorrow morning's rub down will produce he required effect. I guess I'll catch up with you during the day. Steve.

Steve: I think you'll have to wait a long time to get to suck my dick! I really love Mary-Lou, you know. Good luck, all the best for tomorrow - you deserve to win, all the effort you're putting in. Stu.

Stu: Wow, what a weekend. I'm exhausted. It was good to see you and Mary-Lou and really sweet of her to kiss all the slaves like that when you finally found us in the winners' enclosure: it was so spontaneous, so quick, that they barely had time to react to those quick pecks on their cheeks before it was all over! But I know they all thought it was a fantastic gesture, and I could tell they were excited as they all had full erections for about an hour afterwards

They did look great, though, didn't they? They shone with that deep glow from the slave oil, and the way their spiked green hair matched the dray so perfectly? I'd got permission from Jon to have the morning off as potentially winning the competition would be such good publicity for us, but on the morning itself he even allocated another team to come with us! My guys sweated and strained to pick up their dray and put it on the other one, so we could get to the fair grounds without all their hard work in cleaning and polishing the dray being destroyed by the dirt on the roads. And they rode, too - it was a bit hard on the other team, but it also meant that my lot kept their glossy shine. You know, I think this is the first time that my slaves had done anything other than walk and run since they'd been captured and enslaved, so it was pretty novel for them to be sitting there on the dray being pulled along the streets they were so familiar with.

I was right about the "novelty" of entering a dray instead of the usual run of pony carriages, even the big ones that need teams of four to pull them. And of course my "clones" were a sensation, the more so as nine stood there on the dray with his legs spread and his arms above his head holding a big poster advertising our services! It was a bit hard on him, actually - you try standing for an hour in an "X", holding something high in the air, but I'd warned him that any failure was unacceptable and that if he faltered and cost us the prize, not only would I beat the shit out of him but I thought the other slaves would be pretty tough on him, too.

There was that amusing incident, too, when the judge went to pin the first prize rosette somewhere! I guess the pony carriages and stuff usually have some kind of harness or tunic on their slaves, so he was totally at a loss when faced with the nine completely nude slaves of mine. I explained hat they were all so well trained to my voice that there was no need of bits and harnesses, and I think I got a lot of goodwill from him (he's pretty important in the slave trade, and that might be a useful business contact). In the end, I suggested he slip the elastic on the rosette around two's dick and balls, so he was then standing there looking as if he was wearing a fig leaf - I think the judge enjoyed doing it, though, especially a two went so massively hard at the first touch! (I'd forbidden them sex for the past two days, and the slaves were all pretty much on edge). I think the press photographs are really good - all eight of them standing there smiling, two wearing the rosette, and nine crouching in front, still holding up our advertising sign. I was really proud of them, Stu.

After we'd chatted, I was kept pretty busy for the rest of the day talking to people who came past to inspect the winners, and all the slaves were on their best behaviour. Good old two asked me if they could do something special, and for most of the day they trotted up and down the arena giving kids (and their parents, for the very young ones) rides on the dray. We got a huge amount of good will from the public, and I'm sure we'll do additional business as a result. Some old fuddy-duddies did complain to me about the fact that the slaves were almost continuously erect, but although I was polite to them I did have to explain that it didn't matter, as it was only slaves who were on display, after all (I did feel just the tiniest bit guilty about this as in addition to forbidding them sex for the past tow days, I'm mixed some Cialis tablets - those are the things that give old men erections - into their morning feed). I suppose I could have allowed them to jerk off, but there are limits still, I think: the public will tolerate naked slaves, but slaves stroking their dicks in public is still a bit advanced, at least for down here.

When we got back to the depot, the slaves were very tired, but happy. And I fed them a double ration, and gave them slave treats in appreciation. I hung the rosette on the door of their cage so that all the other slaves would know that these guys were champions, as boosting morale like that is so important. But then, as I was about to lock the cage door and leave, I felt so sad - we'd trained together, had a fantastic day as a team, and now I was going to have to leave whereas they could continue celebrating way into the night, together as a team. I think two recognised this, and he said softly to me "Aren't you going to fuck, sir?" and when I said that I thought it was better to leave them all together as they'd want to celebrate with their buddies, he lowered his had and said "but you're part of the team, sir. You're the team leader". Well I think he knew that I knew that he was not telling the entire truth - he was the team leader, whereas I was the manager! He was the sergeant who made it all run smoothly, and I was the officer who gave the orders. He saw my reluctance, and went on "Sir, why don't you join us? You'll be quite safe, sir, I'll see to that."

I trusted him, Stu. I don't suppose there was much real danger actually as any slave who injured or even killed a free man would be put to death immediately and they all knew that. But might they think it was worth a public whipping to gang rape me, for example? Still, I'm pretty impulsive sometimes, as you know, and I did trust two - if he said he'd make sure I was safe, I probably would be. So I stripped off my shirt and shorts, and went into the cage. It was the most amazing night of my life, Stu. I don't know how I can describe to you what it felt like to really be so much part of a team of guys who had really achieved something - it wasn't just the fact of the esprit de corps, or that they were all so happy having had double rations and slave treats, or that they were all primed up and ready for a great night of sex: each of these things was important in itself, but it was the combination of all of them that made it so sensational.

At first I'd felt a bit ashamed, actually, as I knew that my body just couldn't compare to theirs - not even to nine's, as although he'd started off very much like you and me, the exercise and so on had really improved him. So here was I, a skinny, pale guy right in the middle of all these strong, tanned gorgeous hunks - it was like some sot of erotic fantasy I was having. The only way I compared was in the dick department, where you know I've got absolutely nothing to be ashamed of! It was two who really welcomed me, though - he wrapped his arms around me and kissed me, then dropped to his knees to take my dick in his mouth and really excite me until I was leaking pre-cum. Then he gently laid me down in the straw amongst the rest of them and then it was perfectly all right - it felt so great to be surrounded by all these fantastic men, and soon I was rutting away with the rest of them (and, incidentally, showing them that it wasn't only slaves who had the stamina to fuck most of the night!).

I woke up this morning pressed face to face with two, with some other slave's dick pushing at my ass crack. None of them had fucked me, of course, but I just felt so good to have had such a bonding experience. But even as I lay there I knew that this couldn't be - I could allow this one night, this special night, but that discipline demanded that I became once more the manager, the officer. Two saw that I was awake, and I kissed him gently, stroked his dick one last time, then got to my feet and left the cage, locking it behind me (it was pretty irrelevant to lock it at all, actually, as none of the slaves would try to escape really, but we did it to make sure our insurance policy was valid. And, of course, it does remind the slaves that they have no freedom.) I saw him nodding, as he knew that the regular order of things was restored. Steve.

Steve: Wow! And I thought I was having great sex! Look, Steve, we want you to be the first to know. We haven't told anyone else yet - not even my mom and dad. Before I caught the train back to Atlanta on Sunday afternoon I proposed to Mary-Lou, and she accepted me. She's the woman I want to spend the rest of my life with, and there's no point in delaying. I know you'll be happy for us. Stu.

Stu: Wow!, as you say. That's a bit sudden, isn't it? It's so soon after Inga. But yes, of course I'm happy for you, for you both. And, Stu, that's the first time you've done it, I think - you and Mary-Lou are "we" in your note. I think that's a good sign for the future. When's the wedding? I assume you'll want me to be the "best man", and all that stuff about the stag night, and the speech.....? Steve.

Steve: Dad was pretty upset when I called him, after I'd e-mailed you. He wanted me to wait until I'd finished college. And he says, as you did, that it was pretty damned quick after Inga. But the real reason, the unspoken reason, but one we both knew we were hovering around, is that Mary-Lou is not "one of us", not from one of the families in the town with the money and the power. The fact that she's spontaneously happy, has a great personality, gets on well with everyone, and is a joy to be around, seems to be of no consequence compared to the fact that her dad isn't in the Rotary Club, her mom doesn't play at the Bridge Club, and all that other stuff. I hate to say it, Steve, but my parents really are bigots - I know now how it must have felt all those years ago when a guy would have to tell his parents that he wanted to marry a black. Stu.

Stu: Or, more recently, to tell HIS parents that he wasn't going to marry anyone, not ever - for obvious reasons! Steve.

Steve: Dad huffed and puffed and went on and on, and even did the stuff you see in old movies, threatening to cut me off without a penny. But I didn't get cross, and instead played him at his own game - I told him about the way that I needed to "save" myself for marriage, about the lord telling us about the importance of marriage, and all that crap. And that I wasn't strong enough to resist the temptation of the devil (ha, ha.... I hadn't resisted the temptation for one second after I'd met Mary-Lou, as you know!). He tried to pray for me, over the phone, Steve, and it was just as well it was "sound only" as I was able to press the "mute" switch so he couldn't hear me laughing. After about ten minutes I told him that I'd prayed to the lord, and that I'd heard the lord tell me that it was my duty to marry Mary-Lou right now! That's the basic problem with all this religious stuff, isn't it - if you believe in it, someone else can simply lie and you've no way of knowing that as you're so used to just accepting all the religious stuff as the truth! But it worked for me now, and the wedding is going to be in two weeks time - which is just as well, as there's a little Stu on the way. Stu.

Stu: Oh my god! You don't waste any time, do you? Still, you always shot a huge load, and I guess you're pretty fit and fertile.... Many, many congratulations. What do I need to do to get this show on the road? Kiss Mary-Lou for me, and tell her that she can rely on me. And that she'd better be very careful, as if she ever does anything to upset my oldest and best buddy, I'll never forgive her. Steve.

P.S. You're making progress, so the day when as a married man you decide to pick up on "proper" sex again draws closer. I'm waiting! Steve.

(There's a gap in the record here - I seem to remember there was a great flurry on e-mails backwards and forwards as Stu didn't want to miss any classes, and so I had to make most of the arrangements for the wedding. It seemed easier to file all these "wedding" notes in a separate log, and, like all the rest of the stuff, this was destroyed. The one log that survived skips these two weeks, and resumes later.)

Stu: Can I still send notes to you, or are they now to "Mr and Mrs"? There might be some things I want to tell you that I don't want Mary-Lou to hear.

I never though I'd cry at a wedding, and it wasn't just that it felt as if I was losing you, Stu - no, that poem of yours that you had me read out, and then the one that you read to Mary-Lou, had almost the whole congregation in tears. You certainly have a talent for understanding the human condition, and then getting it down on paper. But I can see now that I'm not losing you - it will be different, sure. You know I was worried about that when you were going with Inga, but with Mary-Lou I'm much less worried. You're so clearly happy, Stu, so deliriously, irrationally, totally happy. And Mary-Lou is, too. And when you both hugged me afterwards, it was almost like that incredible night when I truly bonded with my slaves. Steve.

Steve: No, old buddy, you're writing to me. I don't have secrets from Mary-Lou, but there might be things I want to say, too, as you do - or, rather, there may be ways I want to say things - that are best kept private between us. I was touched and moved, Steve, by the way you arranged everything, and by the speech you gave at the reception.

And Mary-Lou and I were truly delighted when we came out of the church and there were all your slaves holding up those floral arches for us to process under - they looked magnificent, with those garlands of fresh flowers hiding their collars and ton ng so well with the bridal flowers. It was a nice touch, too, to have nine backing down the path in front of us strewing rose petals for us to walk on. And this time, when we were to ride together on that dray of yours, you put Mary-Lou in the middle as we made our way to the reception, not as you did with Inga! It certainly was different, all decked out in the flowers to match the slaves' collars - although Mary-Lou says she almost died laughing when she saw your slaves looking faintly embarrassed by those big white satin bows you'd tied around their dicks!

On a more serious note, I think you know that the first poem I read out at the ceremony, where ostens bly I'm talking about friendship and companionship generally, was directed at you? My poem to Mary-Lou was personal, and if things were a little less prejudiced, I'd have made the poem to you personal, too. But we both wanted you to know that we love you, Steve. So every time you read "Thoughts On Friendship", or every time you hear it read out - I feel certain that it's one of my works that will echo on down the years - remember that the "you" in it is YOU, Steve. All our ove. Stu.

Stu: I feel as if my heart is almost breaking. As well as all the preparations for your wedding, I was working away on a proposal and business plan for the way that the whole of our local distribution system ought to be reorganised. Dad wanted me to take it to the Board, and although I had the ideas all in place, getting all the supporting figures and stuff together, and then putting it into a concise presentation, a board-level presentation, was really tough. I'm not used to standing up and speaking in front of a room full of people, either (I don't think your wedding reception counts, as everyone there was so full of love and happiness for you that I could have said anything and they'd still have had tears in their eyes!).

I was really nervous, I can tell you, in that big board room on Fifth Avenue - even though dad had rehearsed me, on the flight up But they accepted it, Stu: the idea that we should go with the new "model" I'd invented of having a ninth slave on the dray to sort the packages and deliver the smaller ones. The savings were so enormous, and the benefits so compelling! Earlier deliveries, and a huge saving from the disposal of surplus slaves as we needed fewer drays, or the avoidance of future costs as purchases of new slaves could be reduced as the business grew.

By the time we got back home, Head Office had already issued implementation instructions, and Jon had begun. We had to lose four drays from that depot, and as my dray would be without a driver because I was to move on, it was one of those chosen: oh yes, I haven't told you - dad was so pleased by the work I'd put in to prepare such a professional business plan that he wants me to go to Harvard, as he says that the future CEO of the company ought to be well educated. Jon had done the other thing I'd recommended, and all the drivers had had to "rank" their slaves from one to eight in terms of their ability to work, their responsiveness, their willingness to obey orders, and so on. Number eight on this scale on each dray was going to be disposed of, and his place "back filled" from some of the slaves on the four totally surplus drays.

A lot of my slaves "survived", Stu, but two was up for disposal! I argued with Jon, but he took me to one side and talked it all through quietly. Although two was a superb worker and was highly valued in organising other slaves, he'd failed disastrously on the ranking for "willingness to obey orders". It was felt that although he did obey, is was more out of personal loyalty to me rather than because of his acceptance of his slavery. Well, I could hardly argue with that, could I? And Jon pointed out that a new driver might not be able to gain that same personal loyalty, and then there would be a potential disaster - so two had to be amongst the slaves they were selling.

I told Jon that I'd buy two as my personal slave, Stu. But he looked at me and said straight out "No, Steve. I know you're pretty headstrong, but take my advice on this one. Listen to me, for once: you're set for great things, I believe. But if you fall for a slave, you'll never achieve your full potential. You need all your energy, all your efforts, to be focussed in the next few years on climbing the corporate ladder - although your dad is a Regional Director, that will make it harder, if anything, rather than easier for you. You don't have time, Steve, to worry about a slave like two. Do you want to get to the end of your life, Steve, and wonder what you might have achieved if you'd only been totally focused?". I wondered what it would feel like to get to the end of my life and wonder what it would have been like to be with two! It was a tough call.

As I left the depot for the last time, as dad had decided I should move to regional head office to see how things worked there before I went to Harvard, two was about to leave, too. He was standing there in the rain, his head bowed in misery, waiting for the slave transporter to take him off to be auctioned. I almost went over to him, but had I done so I know I'd have broken down and gone along with him, and bought him. So I ignored him, Stu. And it was the hardest thing I've ever done. Think of me, alone, and miserable. Steve.

PART 11

Steve and Stu:

The two "s's"! I corresponded with your father almost every day for almost forty years. There were times when we didn't exchange messages for a week or so when I was abroad on a business trip, or your parents were on vacation, but other than that it was pretty much every day until your father's untimely death. The notes we exchanged in those last few weeks when he knew he was dying are some of the most moving things I have ever read, and they have lived in my memory for ever. They were better, or worse, even, than those he sent to me when your mother, Mary-Lou, was killed in that tragedy in Rome where they were vacationing: I doubted his sanity sometimes, so deep was his grief, and wondered if he would ever recover - but from it he left the world possibly his greatest work: "Remembrance"; so perhaps that terrible incident did have at least one positive consequence. Your father and Mary-Lou had the ideal marriage, and in everything he wrote, Stu never once criticised, or complained about anything Mary-Loud did, and their mutual love shone out in every paragraph. I didn't think he could survive her loss, but I think it is generally agreed that some of his finest work came after that, as he wrote and wrote to try to recapture the happiness they had experienced.

When it became obvious that Stu was going to be the finest poet of our generation - some would say the best our country has ever produced - we mutually agreed that we would destroy all the correspondence between us. Our relationship was too precious, and the things we said were sometimes so intimate, that we neither of us wanted them to be picked over by future biographers and students doing doctorates in English. Stu's work stands on its own merits, and does not need "interpreting" in the light of things that were going on in his private life. So the fragment of this enormous correspondence that I have enclosed is all there is, and even though I could perhaps write a personal memoir of Stu, and have been endlessly pressed by biographers and academics alike to do so, I will not. I leave it to you, Steve and Stu, to decide what to do with it. Stu is long since past caring, and I, too, now have only a short time remaining and I am writing this to you to "tidy up" a few loose ends.

Those days of our youth are now so far in the past, but re-reading our e-mails, they seem like yesterday. In my mind I can still see Stu, sitting there in the calm of his study as he read the notes from me; and when I was at the office, or in a hotel room, or at an airport and I read the latest missive from him, I knew I was somehow "at home". I moved around constantly in those early years as I chased promotion, and your father's notes to me were a welcome piece of stability in an otherwise difficult life.

I miss Stu still, miss him dreadfully. And for the past few years, every time I turn on my screen in the morning I still feel a twinge of disappointment that there isn't an e-mail from him waiting for me. It is not appropriate, and not relevant, to tell you whether we ever resumed the "mutual fun" we enjoyed as school kids, and, if we did, whether it ever went beyond mutual jerking off. I'll leave that for the biographers to speculate over.

I will however tell you that Stu did one extraordinary act of friendship, that went far, far beyond anything that anyone has a right to expect. You will know that I like men, and I have never made any secret of it. It did not ever affect my career, and when I joined the company, I swiftly and ruthlessly rose through the ranks. On dad's death I used my inheritance to buy a further substantial tranche of company stock, and thus got myself elected to the Board. Once there, it was a much smaller step to be appointed CEO, and then, in what is still talked about as the coup of the century, I staked everything on raising an enormous loan in conjunction with a private equity investment house, to buy out the stockholders and take the company private. I am, and have been for many years, the sole owner of all the trucks, planes, office buildings and slaves who make up the country's largest - some would say only - distributor. I propose to pay back your father's generosity by leaving the company to you two, and my doctors tell me that it will now be but a short time before you will inherit. I've had a long and interesting life, and I will not regret leaving it now as it is so tiresome to be so weary all the time - but take care of that which I built.

That act of generosity was to give me a son. Your mother agreed to accept some of my semen to give me that which I most desired - a son to carry my genes on to future generations. She and Stu and I discussed it at length when they heard I was planning to buy a female slave and have her inseminated, and they persuaded me from this course of action by pointing out that children should grow up in loving homes, where parents could cherish and guide them. As I was still forging my career I would not have time, and a slave was hardly suitable to be entrusted with parenting. Over the years I have seen you both grow and mature, and your parents truly did an excellent job: you are both so confident and mature that only this background could have given you these tremendous gifts. I was in favour of keeping your parentage secret, but Stu and Mary-Lou would have none of it, and so I know that this revelation is not a complete shock to you. And, with my "special" knowledge, I think I detected that as half brothers you were not inhibited from truly bonding with each other in a way that only men can.

The only regret I have is "two". What would have happened if, defying convention, I had bought him that next week at the auction? We'll never know, of course. But you have two close examples of how to live your lives: your parents, who lived for love and where Stu only achieved fame and fortune as he neared death; and me, who lived for his career, and who had both fame and fortune from an early age but who never really had a close relationship - except for the written one with Stu.

Think closely about your objectives in life. You will never lack for money. You have the huge advantage of having been loved, and of knowing love for each other. Would I do things differently if, by some chance, there really is a juju waiting for me in the sky who grants me a second opportunity? I don't know. Would I stop at the gate, gently brush the rain off two's skin, and tell him not to worry as he would spend but a short time caged at the auction house before he was once more my trusted "sergeant"? Sometimes I replay that scene in my mind and spin tales and dreams of the life we might have had together. Would I trade what I did achieve for that chance of happiness? I still don't know.

Nothing I ever did subsequently - none of the important jobs, none of the boardroom coups, none of the major deals - ever really gave me the satisfaction that I got when, at nineteen, I won the County Fair competition: I sometimes think that was the crowning achievement of my life. And none of the rewards with which I have been showered were ever as satisfying as the way the slaves showed me their devotion that night. If you get to my age and you can say that you had one true friend, and you did just one thing that you remember for ever, you will be truly fortunate. But perhaps it is different for half brothers, who have had the opportunity to grow up together and discover for themselves the strength of the ties that can bond one man to another. Continue to love each other, as your father and I loved each other, and be happy.

Tears are filling my eyes as rereading the correspondence has been both painful and joyous, rather as sex can be. Do as you will with the correspondence - I now no longer need it, and soon both the main protagonists will be dead, and I imagine the slaves are long gone as their work will have worn them out. Not that that is a real consideration as they were, after all, however much I liked them, slaves. But then, how much did I really know them? It was only nine whose name I even knew, and two was always just that to me - his real name, his family, his own life, were always unknown - and so he must remain just "two". Who knows - one of his sons, as I believe he had sired children before enslavement - may even read this memoir, should you choose to publish it.

For the last time, as typing is now so tiring. Steve.

ABOUT THE AUTHOR

Pete Brown is a very busy man who lives in London and loves to write about how he wished he lived.

Pete Brown is also the author of **The Toy**. This book and many more available at Amazon.com, TheNazcaPlainsCorp.com or your local bookstore.

the

Toy

a novel by

PETE BROWN

A BONER BOOK